P9-DFY-398

"You've had a comfortable life. Some of us weren't so lucky."

Instead of revealing background information that was none of James Harris's business, Megan merely said, "It's not luck. It's a choice. I look at life's roadblocks as opportunities to triumph over adversity."

Her smile grew to a full-blown grin as her glance traveled from his booted feet to the top of his head. "And you, mister, are about as *big* a roadblock as I've ever had to overcome. The time we're about to spend working together with the camp children and my animals should be very challenging."

"Now *that* we agree on."

Books by Valerie Hansen

Love Inspired

*The Wedding Arbor #84
*The Troublesome Angel #103
*The Perfect Couple #119
*Second Chances #139
*Love One Another #154
*Blessings of the Heart #206
*Samantha's Gift #217
*Everlasting Love #270

*Serenity, Arkansas

VALERIE HANSEN

was thirty when she awoke to the presence of the Lord in her life and turned to Jesus. In the years that followed she worked with young children, both in church and secular environments. She also raised a family of her own and played foster mother to a wide assortment of furred and feathered critters.

Married to her high school sweetheart since age seventeen, she now lives in an old farmhouse she and her husband renovated with their own hands. She loves to hike the wooded hills behind the house and reflect on the marvelous turn her life has taken. Not only is she privileged to reside among the loving, accepting folks in the breathtakingly beautiful Ozark Mountains of Arkansas, she also gets to share her personal faith by telling the stories of her heart for Steeple Hill's Love Inspired line.

EVERLASTING LOVE

VALERIE HANSEN

Steeple
Hill®

Published by Steeple Hill Books™

If you purchased this book without a cover you should be aware
that this book is stolen property. It was reported as "unsold and
destroyed" to the publisher, and neither the author nor the
publisher has received any payment for this "stripped book."

STEEPLE HILL BOOKS

Steeple
Hill®

ISBN 0-373-87280-1

EVERLASTING LOVE

Copyright © 2004 by Valerie Whisenand

All rights reserved. Except for use in any review, the reproduction
or utilization of this work in whole or in part in any form by any
electronic, mechanical or other means, now known or hereafter
invented, including xerography, photocopying and recording, or in
any information storage or retrieval system, is forbidden without
the written permission of the editorial office, Steeple Hill Books,
233 Broadway, New York, NY 10279 U.S.A.

All characters in this book have no existence outside the imagination of
the author and have no relation whatsoever to anyone bearing the same
name or names. They are not even distantly inspired by any individual
known or unknown to the author, and all incidents are pure invention.

This edition published by arrangement with Steeple Hill Books.

® and TM are trademarks of Steeple Hill Books, used under license.
Trademarks indicated with ® are registered in the United States Patent
and Trademark Office, the Canadian Trade Marks Office and in other
countries.

www.SteepleHill.com

Printed in U.S.A.

Moreover, let us also be full of joy now!
Let us exult and triumph in our troubles and
rejoice in our sufferings, knowing that pressure
and affliction and hardship produce patience
and unswerving endurance.

—*Romans* 5:3

To Manda, whose trials have been many,
especially lately, and who has
all my love and prayers

Chapter One

Megan White was annoyed with herself for feeling apprehensive. This was the chance of a lifetime. She should be ecstatic. Appreciative of all the blessings involved. Thrilled to have the opportunity to help her teenage sister, Roxanne, as well as the homeless kids they were about to meet. And she *was* glad. Really. She just needed to keep reminding herself to be thankful for everything, even her brooding companion.

Sighing, she glanced over at Roxy. The fifteen-year-old had relaxed some since she'd picked her up at their mother's house, but Megan could tell there was still a huge chip on the girl's shoulder.

"Hey, look at this great weather," Megan said cheerfully. "We couldn't ask for a prettier day."

Roxy merely grunted.

"And the beautiful dogwood trees. Wow! Don't you just love the Ozarks?"

"I guess."

Megan paused a moment, then plunged ahead, following her heart. "Look, Roxy, I know this trip wasn't your idea, but that doesn't mean we can't make the best of it. It'll be fun. You'll see."

The girl's head whipped around. Her expression was half stoicism, half vulnerability. "You don't have to do this, Meg. All I want is to get away from Dad's new wife and her snotty kid for a little while. I could stay with Mom if she'd take me back. How long do I have to pay for going to live with Dad? All my life?"

"We can't change the past, honey. I'm trying to make things better for you. So is Mom. It was hard on all of us when they got divorced."

"Yeah, but you could go off to college. I was stuck."

"I'm sorry if you felt I was ducking our problems instead of sharing them with you."

Roxanne's eyes widened. "How did you know?"

"I'm a psych major, remember?"

"You think that makes you smarter? You don't have any idea what it was like for me after Dad decided to marry that witch. Her kid was supposed to be some kind of perfect angel. I couldn't do anything right."

"Remember those feelings when you're talking to some of the kids we're going to meet. Compared to the kind of stuff they've been through, you and I've had it easy. We started out with both parents and a nice place to live. Lots of them never had anything like that."

"I won't know what to say."

"Just be kind. Be their friend. Working with my therapy animals should take care of the rest." *And maybe heal your broken heart the way they've healed mine.*

Mulling over the events of the past few hectic days, Megan realized the answer to her concerns about her sister had dropped right in her lap. She just hoped she'd be able to properly fulfill her original objective while helping Roxy at the same time.

She smiled. Of course she would. It wasn't chance that had brought her sister to her at such a perfect time, any more than it was an accident that a stray kitten had entered her life when she was a lonely, confused teen like Roxy. That sweet kitten had loved unconditionally and provided Megan's first insights into the work she was now doing. All she had to do was continue to follow the good Lord's leading and everything would turn out fine.

Such a lofty conclusion made her chuckle. The perfect Christian was yet to be found and she wasn't even close. Knowing human nature, she'd be lucky to get through her short stint at Camp Refuge without making bunches of mistakes.

Good thing even the most fallible people got some things right, wasn't it? Otherwise, nothing worthwhile would ever be accomplished.

Amazed and pleased that she'd located the camp so effortlessly, Megan pulled through the gateway. She slowed her pickup truck, peering out at the old wooden cabins and deserted play areas.

She'd chosen Camp Refuge because it reportedly housed only a few wards of the court at one time and she'd wanted to limit the number of children she had to chart for her thesis, but this place looked too desolate.

Roxy noticed, too. "Where is everybody?"

"I don't know. Maybe I got the wrong camp."

"Nope. The sign out front said this is it."

"Okay, I'll keep going."

Following the dirt road deeper into the complex, Megan noticed a tall, dark-haired man standing in front of what looked like the main building.

He'd apparently been anticipating her arrival because he started to amble toward the truck before she'd come to a complete stop. Then he looked up, smiled slightly—and took her breath away.

It wasn't an inappropriate smile. Certainly not a come-on. Yet the mountain air seemed suddenly insufficient. Megan had to work hard to appear unaffected.

Roxanne had no such qualms. "Wow. Maybe I *am* going to like it here."

"Down, girl. This is strictly business, remember?"

"For you, maybe. I'm just along for the ride."

"Oh, no, you're not. I brought you because you're a natural with animals. I really do need your help."

"I know, I know. Don't have a fit. I'll be good, Meg. But I'm not dead. And that is one great-looking guy, even if he is way too old for me."

"Can't argue with that," Megan said with a knowing grin. She put the truck in park and killed the engine. "Guess I'd better go introduce myself. You wait here."

"Do I have to?"

"Yes. Until I explain who you are and why you're with me, I think I should be the one to do all the talking."

"Like, I can't talk?"

"Nooooo. Like, I'm the adult."

"Bossy, bossy."

If Roxy hadn't been smiling, Megan would have been more concerned about their sibling relationship. The younger girl had grown up a lot while Megan had been away at college and there were areas of both their lives that had changed.

She paused and tried to swallow past the dryness in her throat. "I'll be right back. I promise."

"You nervous?"

"Naw. I always shake like this."

"How come you're scared?"

"I'm not scared. Not exactly. It's just that this project is very important to me. I want to make a good first impression."

"You will. You've always been the brainy one. Go impress him, sis."

"Thanks, I will…I hope."

Comparing her equilibrium to that of a formerly sturdy table that had just had one of its four legs sawed off, Megan stepped down out of the truck, slammed the door, tossed back her shoulder-length hair and smoothed the hem of her T-shirt before she turned. Then she boldly stepped forward to meet the man she was to work with for the next two weeks.

Smile bright and eager, she offered her hand. "Hi. I'm Megan White."

"James Harris," he said pleasantly. "Welcome to Camp Refuge."

"Thanks. I'm happy to finally be here and meet you face-to-face, Mr. Harris. After we spoke on the phone the other day, I wasn't sure what kind of reception I'd get."

"Really?" One dark eyebrow arched.

Oops. She chewed her lower lip, ruing her candid comment and wishing she could take it back. *Oh, good one, Megan,* she thought. *Put him on the defensive right off, why don't you? Way to go.*

Questions remained in his deep brown eyes as he shook her hand. Megan was thankful their handshake was brief. A few more seconds of that man's warm touch and she was afraid she'd have felt like a second table leg had been sawed off!

"Are you always so honest?" James asked.

"I hope not," she said with a nervous chuckle.

His resulting laughter was hearty and genuine.

Megan's stomach did an immediate flip-flop and landed in her throat where it could keep close company with her racing heart. Her project was already getting too complicated, thanks to the addition of a moody assistant. Finding that the camp director was neither old nor ugly, as she'd imagined, just added to her problems. Roxy was feeling abandoned and unloved. The poor kid was primed to develop a crush on the first good-looking guy who was nice to her, and in the case of this particular man, Megan could see how easily that could happen.

Well, there was nothing to do but forge ahead. "I brought my sister with me. She'll be a big help with the animals. I hope you don't mind."

He leaned to peer past her into the truck. "Sister? I wasn't expecting two of you."

"I know. Sorry for the inconvenience. We'll bunk together, of course. I'll be totally responsible."

"Yes, you will. How old is she?"

"Fifteen. She's a great kid. You'll like her."

He looked again. "You're not twins?"

Megan blushed under his steady assessment. "No. I assure you I'm much older."

"Could have fooled me. Same dark hair, same pale skin. Don't see that much around here, not with all the sun we get in the summer."

"Our mom is light and Daddy is kind of dark," she explained, nervously combing her hair back with her fingers and tucking the sides smoothly behind her ears. "Roxy can get a pretty tan. I always burn. But enough about us. I want to thank you for letting me bring my project here."

"Don't thank me," James said. "Like I told you when you phoned, I think these kids have enough troubles already. They don't need more grief."

"I agree. But my animals have been chosen and trained to be particularly gentle and loving. What makes you think being around them will have a negative effect?"

"Experience," he said flatly. "These kids are only here for a short time. They already get too attached to me and my staff for their own good. Imagine how hard it will be for some of the more sensitive ones to leave a favorite pet behind, too."

This was the kind of unreasonable attitude Megan had battled more than once. "Have you bothered to read my formal proposal, Mr. Harris?"

"I scanned it enough to get the basics. I don't need to read all the details to see it has problems you haven't even considered. I know what'll happen. I have plenty of firsthand experience working with troubled kids."

"And I suppose they all respond to your methods?" she asked. "None of your students resist reform?"

The brief flash of emotion in his deep brown eyes took her aback. So did a surge of compassion. She hadn't meant to belittle his work or hurt his feelings; she'd merely wanted to make him listen to reason and give her project a fair shake. She needed an ally, not an adversary.

"I'm sorry. I shouldn't have said that," Megan told him. "I know this camp has done a lot of good. But there must be children no one's been able to reach by normal methods. Kids who've been so battered by their pasts that they've withdrawn from everybody and everything. Isn't that so?"

James gave a reluctant nod, shrugged and stuffed his hands into his pockets. "Yes. Of course."

"Then you should be glad to have me around. It's not like it's forever, you know. When I wrote my proposal for the grant, I designed it to cover a short period of time."

"I know that. I also know these kids."

"I can help them."

"Can you? They come and go around here like they're stuck in a revolving door. They need peace, not some do-gooder trying to run them through a maze like lab rats."

Megan was appalled. "If you'd read my entire proposal you wouldn't say that. All I'm planning to do is introduce a few docile animals into their lives, to give them a nonjudgmental friend to care for and confide in. You talk like I'm planning to throw defenseless kids to a pack of lions."

"It could end up being the reverse of that," James warned. "Have you stopped to consider the welfare of your animals? Or of your sister?"

"What do you mean?"

"This isn't a church camp anymore. It's a way station for kids who have no place else to go. They've been bucking the system for so long, they don't know how to behave in a normal family environment."

"I understand that."

"Do you also understand how cruel they can be for no apparent reason? I can't guarantee absolute safety."

Megan huffed as she gave him a brief once-over. The man was obviously strong as an ox. Moreover, now that she'd had time to observe him, she'd noticed a hard, militarylike edge that gave him the kind of commanding presence few people questioned.

She, however, refused to be cowed. "You look like you can handle just about any situation, Mr. Harris. With your support, I'm sure we won't have any trouble."

"Exactly my point, Ms. White," he said, raising an eyebrow and folding his arms across his chest. "I can't be everywhere at once. And even if I could, I don't have time to baby-sit you or your little sister. Bringing more unknown elements into these kids' already-muddled lives is about the dumbest idea I think I've ever heard."

Blinking in disbelief, she suddenly giggled. "Hey, don't hold back, mister. Feel free to speak up. Give me your honest opinion."

"I thought I just did."

"That was a joke, Harris." She shook her head and continued to chuckle. "Okay. Have it your way. I prefer to focus on the good stuff."

"You would. You've had a comfortable life. Some of us weren't so lucky."

Instead of revealing background information that was none of his business, Megan merely said, "It's not luck. It's a choice. I look at life's roadblocks as opportunities to triumph over adversity."

Her smile grew to a full-blown grin as her glance traveled from his booted feet to the top of his head. "And you, mister, are about as *big* a roadblock as I've ever had to overcome. The time we're about to spend working together should be very challenging."

"Now *that* we agree on."

It amused her to watch the corners of his mouth twitch while he struggled to stifle a smile. She laughed lightly, her mood beginning to confirm her innate spirit of joy. "I'll want to speak to the rest of your staff, of course, but that can wait until I've brought my animals and set up their compound. First, I'd like to look the place over, pick out a cabin and start moving in."

She gestured toward the back of her truck. A bright blue tarp was stretched over the bed to weatherproof it. "We didn't bring much personal gear this trip because I didn't know what was available up here. We mostly need a place with enough outside clearance to set up my portable corrals and a few smaller pens. Nothing fancy."

"You're really going to go through with this?"

"Of course, I am." She shot him an incredulous look. "Was there ever any doubt?"

Starting back toward the truck to fetch Roxy, Megan sensed him following, then heard him mumble, "Apparently not."

Though the words were meant to sound grumpy, she could tell from his tone that he'd finally given in to the smile he'd been trying so hard to suppress. That was definitely a plus. As a mature woman, she was immune to his charms, of course. She just hoped he didn't smile too amiably at her impressionable sister. At fifteen, a girl could fall in love in seconds—or at least believe she had.

Megan was far wiser than that. She'd had plenty of chances to find a mate in college, yet had managed to keep her distance. No way was she going to let fleeting romance jeopardize her opportunity for a formal education. That was what her mother had done, and look what had happened. The woman was alone, uneducated and working for minimum wage, while her ex was earning big bucks and starting a new family.

As Megan saw it, marriage was the least likely way to find bliss, whereas independence meant living life exactly the way she wanted. She was no starry-eyed kid who thought she had to have a man in her life in order to be happy. Her happiness came from using her God-given talents to help others. That was plenty.

Chapter Two

With Megan in the lead and Roxy hanging back to chatter at James, they passed cabin after cabin, standing vacant amid the oak, walnut and sycamore trees of the old-growth forest. The mountain air was fresh and clear. Birds sang and flitted above, and in the distance Megan could hear the soft rush of the Spring River. What she didn't hear was children at play.

Shading her eyes with one hand, she paused to peer between the trees, then looked to James. "Where is everybody, anyway?"

"Inside, catching up with schoolwork they missed. Our census is down. We're licensed to take up to thirty wards of the court at one time. Fortunately, there are only six boys in residence now."

He pointed down the hill. "When we have girls to look after, they bunk in that cabin over there, usually with Inez Gogerty. She and her sister take turns cooking for us and staying the night if we need extra female chaperones. As long as there's no open conflict between the boys, they all get to live in the same cabin."

"Does that happen a lot? Fighting, I mean."

"No. Not often. If it does, I take charge of the quarrelsome ones and assign the others to Aaron Barnes. He's a college student who helps me out whenever I need him. I try not to call him too often, though. The more money I can save the tax-payers, the more kids I can afford to help."

Megan arched her eyebrows. She didn't doubt the man's veracity. It was just that her grant was going to provide extra help, at no cost to Camp Refuge or the state of Arkansas, and yet he wasn't willing to accept her with open arms. *Figuratively speaking, of course.*

"I want to help children, too, you know," she said.

"I know you do. Why don't you take your project and sell it to somebody who really needs it?"

"Like who?"

He shrugged his wide shoulders, reminding Megan of a high school football player Roxy had

had a terrible crush on. Only, James Harris didn't need any extra padding to make his frame formidable looking, did he?

Now stop that! Appalled at the way her thoughts kept straying to his physical attractiveness, Megan quickly reminded herself that appropriate Christian behavior did not include daydreaming about a man, let alone one she'd just met!

James drew her back into their conversation by asking, "How about handicapped children?"

"What? Oh…" She blinked rapidly to clear her head, happy to tell him more about her work. "Been there, done that. Actually, it was my undergraduate work with a special needs group that prompted me to do my thesis on using animals for emotional therapy. You may as well give it up, Harris. Your board of trustees is on my side, one hundred percent."

"So I've gathered. Care to explain how you managed that? Those three idiotic old codgers haven't agreed on anything in twenty years."

"Thirty," Megan said, watching the camp director's face closely. "At least that's what my college mentor told me when he suggested I propose my project to the other two."

"Other two? Your mentor is on the board?"

"He sure is. Any more questions?"

"No, just give me a second to get my foot out of my mouth," James said, ignoring Roxy's giggling as he continued to address Megan. "I hope you don't plan to tell the man I said he was an old codger."

"I don't intend to say one single derogatory thing about you or this camp. Not as long as you give me your full cooperation."

"Blackmail?"

"Of course not," Megan insisted with a wry look, intending it to be more telling than her denial. "We're two intelligent adults who both want what's best for some troubled kids. When I make my final report to the board, I'm sure they'll be pleased at how well we've worked together." She boldly thrust her hand toward him. "Shake on it, partner?"

Time crept by slower than an ant on an ice cube. There was clearly a dandy struggle going on in that good-looking head of his. When one corner of his mouth quirked with the hint of a smile, however, Megan knew she'd won.

Nodding, James grasped her outstretched hand and cupped his other hand over it. "Okay. Partners. As long as you don't butt heads with me in front of the kids and undermine my authority, I'll put up with you. Both of you. But one false move and you're out of here. I don't care if you have friends in high places all over Arkansas. Is that understood?"

"Uh-huh."

Dumbfounded, she stared at their clasped hands. His touch was warm, comforting, gentle. Her skin was tingling worse than the first time they'd shared a handshake. Much worse. A shiver began at the nape of her neck and skittered along her spine, confirming the full extent of her reaction to James's innocent touch.

This was more serious than her earlier tendencies to admire his looks. And a lot more scary. Emotions were her business. She recognized the signs all too well. Apparently, some of the uneasiness she'd attributed to simple nervousness when she'd first met him had had its roots elsewhere in her psyche.

Megan pulled her hand free. The effects of James's touch lingered, making her pulse race. Worse yet, her impressionable sister was standing right there, watching the whole exchange and giving her the kind of look a parent gives a child who's been caught raiding the cookie jar.

Embarrassed, Megan swallowed hard. This was not good. Not good at all. There was more at stake here than simply preserving her own peace of mind. Preaching to Roxy about virtuous behavior was not going to have any effect if she couldn't set a good example, both in practice and in her heart of hearts.

Megan knew her actions were not going to be too hard to manage, especially if she relied on prayer for extra support. It was her errant *thoughts* that were going to give her fits. Thanks to meeting James Harris, wild notions were already spinning around in her head like dry leaves caught in a whirlwind.

The cabin Megan eventually chose was not among the ones James had hoped she'd pick. Naturally. He gritted his teeth. Leave it to her to fixate on a building that had stood empty for years. He'd been associated with Camp Refuge for nearly a decade, first as a part-timer, then as a counselor and finally as its director, and he couldn't recall a time when anyone had occupied the small, outlying cabin. It certainly wasn't appealing, yet the woman seemed unreasonably drawn to it.

"Are you *sure?*" he asked for the third time.

"Positive." She led the way up onto the porch, looking down and frowning. "You'll need to repair these steps. They feel wobbly. I hope the interior is in better shape."

"I can't promise a thing. We haven't used this row of cabins for anything but storage for years. Why does it have to be this one? There are lots better choices closer to our main bunkhouses and dining hall."

"Because I *like* this one," Megan insisted. "It has a big enough yard for my horse pen. Plus, my rabbits will need plenty of shade. These trees will be perfect for that. Right, Roxy?"

The teenager shrugged. "Whatever."

Frustrated, James stared at Megan. "Did you get up this morning determined to do everything the hard way? Or is it simply a talent of yours to be difficult?"

She laughed softly. "I have lots of special gifts, but I've never been told making trouble is one of them."

"Well, let me be the first," he said, turning the front-door key. "This lock is sticking, too. I'll need to make a list of repairs. It'll be a long one."

"Don't go to any fuss. I can take care of whatever needs to be done inside. Roxy can help me dust and sweep the place out. It'll be fine."

"I doubt that."

Pushing open the door on creaking hinges, he

stood back so the others could peek into the interior. As he'd suspected, the cabin not only smelled musty, it was chock-full of items that had been stored for so long, their value was nil. The stacks of cardboard file boxes were bad enough. Worse, extra cots had been piled along one whole wall. From the looks of the bundles of old mattresses, they'd been home to families of field mice for some time.

Megan made a face. Clearly ignoring her sister's muffled squeal of protest she said, "Hmmm. This could take a bit more than dusting."

"Exactly." James started to pull the door closed. "So, what's your second choice?"

"I don't have one. I want this cabin."

"You must be kidding."

"No. Not at all. Like I said, it's perfect for my needs. Think you can have the junk out of it by Monday?"

He rolled his eyes. This woman was not only stubborn beyond reason, she was also nuts. "Monday? Of next month, maybe. This is already Friday. There's no way I can spare the time to do the hours of work this place will need. It's impossible."

"Nothing is impossible if you want it badly enough," Megan argued. "And I want this cabin. If you can't clean it out, we'll do it ourselves."

"No way! Not me." Roxy retreated and scurried down the porch steps.

All James could do was shake his head. He'd never met anyone as inflexible as Megan White. Nor anyone so determined. How did all that stubbornness fit into such a compact package? When he'd been tossed out by his parents and shipped off to military school as a young teen, he'd thought those instructors were unbelievably rigid. But they'd been softies compared to this woman.

"I can't let you do that." He cast around for a plausible excuse, settling on "It's against camp policy" before he realized she'd be privy to the details of actual camp policy through her mentor.

"I'm starting to get the idea you don't want us here," Megan chided, breaking into a silly grin. "Well, you can forget about scaring us off. Roxy and I are moving in on Monday, with or without your help. Now, where do you want us to put all this junk after we drag it out the door?"

He knew when he was licked. "Okay, okay. I'll help you. Let me go get the old dump truck we use to haul trash. We can back it up to the porch and toss stuff into it from there so we won't have to handle anything twice. I have a bad feeling this place is loaded with spiders, not to mention other crawly things."

It pleased him to note Megan's barely perceptible shiver. She'd listened to that warning, at least. He was in favor of anything that fostered caution and slowed her momentum. Which gave him another idea.

"You could be settled in one of the regular cabins down the hill in a few hours, you know. Today."

When she whirled to face him, hands fisted on her slim hips, she didn't have to say a word to inform him his sensible suggestion had been in vain.

He shook his head in resignation. "Okay, okay. You win. I'll go tell Inez and Aaron to keep watching the kids for me and I'll get the truck. Don't try to move anything until I get back. Understand?"

"Perfectly."

As he started away, Roxy hurried to match his stride. He slowed for her. "Aren't you going to stay and help your big sister?"

"No way. That place is too creepy. I don't do spiders. Or windows, either."

"I don't blame you for hating spiders," he said soberly. "I'm not real crazy about them myself."

"Are you married?"

James faltered and almost tripped. "No. Why?"

"Just wondered."

"Are you asking for yourself, or did your sister put you up to it?"

"Her? Naw." Roxy made a face. "Meg doesn't care. She's never had lots of dates like I have. I'm a cheerleader, you know. Varsity."

"Congratulations."

"Thanks. How old are the boys who live here?"

"Younger than you," he said dryly. "And while we're on the subject, I want you to understand something. These kids are already confused and worried when they come to camp. If you do or say anything to upset them further, I'll have to end your sister's project early and send you both away. Is that clear?"

Roxy shrugged. "Sure. It's not my problem. I'm only here because my mother didn't want to be bothered with me."

"I thought you came to help Megan."

"Whatever. It wasn't my idea."

Thoughtful, James refrained from further comment. He hadn't been crazy about the idea of bringing animals into the camp in the first place. Now that Megan had added a troubled teen to the mix, he was even less inclined to endorse the project.

It's only for fourteen days, he reminded himself. *Two weeks.* Surely, not much could go wrong in that short a time.

When James returned with the dump truck he was alone. He handed Megan some leather gloves and donned a matching pair. "Your sister decided to stay with Inez."

"Not a big surprise." The gloves were miles too big. Nevertheless, Megan expressed gratitude as she put them on. "Thanks. It was nice of you to think of bringing these for me. If I'd known I was going to be doing a lot of manual labor today I'd have come better prepared."

"You're welcome. There's bottled water in the cab of the truck, too. I don't want you using the taps in the cabin until I've had a chance to flush them out. Might make you sick."

"Aren't you sweet? Thanks."

"Me? Sweet?" He chuckled. "You're the first person who's ever called me *that*."

Slightly disconcerted, he reached for a stack of cardboard boxes, looking them over carefully while brushing away spiderwebs with one gloved hand. "All these old records are in our computer system so it'll be okay to pitch them. I'd forgotten this stuff was still around."

"You've worked here a long time?"

"On and off. I started volunteering when I was still in school. After I got my degree, I went into teaching but it wasn't satisfying enough. I finally chucked it all and came back here to stay. Been here ever since."

Megan nodded. "Why don't you do the heavy work and leave those boxes to me? I can move them by myself if I only lift one or two at a time. I know I can't handle the mattresses." Pointing, she gifted him with her most convincing smile. "Please?"

"Okay." James straightened. "Just keep your gloves on and watch out for spiders. We have a lot of brown recluse up here. I fight them all the time in the bunkhouses."

"You be careful, too. Looks like the wasps have taken over that end of the cabin."

"Mud daubers. They're everywhere, especially in attics. Chances are they even managed to find a way into some of those boxes you're about to handle."

"Terrific." She made a silly face at him.

"Hey, you're the one who insisted on doing this. I'm still willing to be sensible."

"No way." It amused Megan to see him giving her a look that said he thought she was dumber than a post. She laughed softly. "I discovered a long time ago that the only way to be sure you'll lose is to quit before you reach your goal. That's why I never give up. It's not in my nature."

"Not even if you're fighting a losing battle?" James asked as he dragged a huge bundle of dilapidated mattresses toward the door.

"In whose opinion? Yours? Mine? That's not nearly good enough for me."

Watching him work, Megan couldn't help continuing to appreciate his natural appeal. Not that she ever intended to reveal her thoughts. Or act on them. She simply had an ingrained admiration for all of God's creatures. And she had to admit this particular creature was pretty close to perfect, at least on the outside. What was inside was the problem. He'd looked after her by providing gloves and drinking water, sure, but his lack of open-mindedness spoiled his overall image.

"So," he asked, "what does it take to influence you? A lightning bolt from heaven?"

"Something like that."

The dust they'd stirred up was making her nose tickle. She slipped off one glove and pressed her clean forefinger against her upper lip to stifle a sneeze. "Sometimes it feels like the good Lord has to drop a brick on my head to get my attention. Once He does, I try to listen before the second brick comes along."

"Does that happen often?"

"Fortunately, no," Megan said, "or I'd have to go into the chimney-building business." She sneezed twice and sniffled. "As anyone will tell you, I'm just about flawless by now."

Her quip, coupled with the look of disbelief on his face as he turned away, made her giggle.

James made it as far as the back of the truck before he, too, began to sneeze. Repeatedly. By this time, Megan had joined him on the porch with the first of the storage boxes.

Her next "Achoo!" blew a puff of fine dust off the top of the box and left them standing with their heads in a cloud of it. "Sorry. I guess I must be allergic to whatever's in this dirt."

"You and me both," James said. "I should have thought of that. My allergies aren't usually too bad this time of year. It slipped my mind."

Heaving the bundle of mattresses into the truck bed he followed it with the box Megan had been holding, then jumped down off the porch. "Stay put. Don't move anything else till I get back. I've got a couple of disposable masks left over from when I painted the dorm. Wearing those should help. Anything'll be better than sneezing our heads off like this."

"Bring a box of tissues, too. And if you run into my sister, tell her I'm just about ready to send her home to face the music."

"She might like that. She said she didn't want to come with you in the first place."

"True." Megan stifled another sneeze. "This

trip was the best of her options though, even if she won't admit it."

"I don't want any trouble here," James warned.

"There won't be. Roxy's as sweet-natured as she is pretty. She just needed to get away from home for a while. I expect her to be a lot of help to me."

James chuckled, glanced down the hill and said, between sneezes, "Oh, yeah? When?"

By the time James returned, Megan had discovered an abandoned mouse nest and had deposited it on the porch.

Handing her the box of tissues and one of the white paper masks, he scowled at the matted nest. "I told you to wait for me."

"I did. Sort of."

"Then what's that?"

"Well, it's not the latest in porch decor," she quipped with a smile. "I prefer pots of petunias, myself."

He eyed the jumbled mass of leaves, twigs, fabric and mattress ticking. "What'd you do with the mice that lived in there, make pets of them?"

There was something about his glib attitude that brought out her sense of rivalry, made her want to best him, wit to wit. "I would have, if they'd been around when I found their house. I thought I'd teach them to ride tiny bicycles and juggle little balls, maybe made out of dried peas. I could paint the peas bright colors. They'd be lovely. What do you think?"

James slowly shook his head and looked down to hide his smile. "Believe me, you don't want to know what I think."

"You're probably right about that. So, shall we put on our masks and dive in again?"

"No. I'll do it alone," he said. "You just stand here and hold the door for me."

"The door is fine. It doesn't need holding."

"Put on your mask so you don't eat any more dust and do as I say."

"In a pig's eye."

"Don't tell me you have a pet pig, too."

"Nope. Just a horse, a burro, a couple of rabbits, a herding dog and Rocky."

James had already donned his mask, which muffled his reply, but Megan got a general idea of what he was asking so she explained, "Rocky's a flying squirrel. I rescued him from a tree that had been cut down when he was just a baby. I've tried to release him back into the wild but he keeps coming home and sneaking into the house. Apparently, he likes living in my menagerie."

"Guess there's no accounting for taste."

"When you're right, you're right." Megan put on her paper mask and went back inside.

Removing the stored supplies didn't take nearly as long as Megan had thought it would. Cleaning the cabin until it looked and smelled as fresh as a summer breeze, however, took her and James the rest of the afternoon.

Finished, she plopped down on the edge of the small porch and dangled her feet over the side. "Whew! I'm bushed. We used up *all* the cleanser you brought."

"You should be tired. You worked hard."

There was a tinge of admiration in his voice. She leaned her head back to glance up at him. "Hey, if I impressed you, it was worth it."

"You did. So, what's next? When are you going to bring the animals and set up your zoo?"

"It's not a zoo."

"Whatever. I'd just like to know if I should expect any other big surprises."

"Big? Like what? An elephant?"

His eyes widened. "Tell me you're kidding."

"Okay. I'm kidding."

James heaved a sigh and joined her. "That's a relief."

Pretending to make room for him, Megan inched farther away for her own sake and feigned a lighthearted attitude. "Sorry if I scared you. Guess you're not used to my crazy sense of humor."

"Guess not." He took a deep breath and let it out with a whoosh as he stretched his arms and shoulders. "Why don't you and Roxy stay and have supper with me and the boys? Inez always cooks extra."

"Looking like this?" Megan eyed her dusty clothing. Her jeans and shirt were filthy. So were her bare arms. She hated to think what her hair looked like, not to mention the grime that had to be all over her face. "I don't want to scare the kids, too."

"They don't scare as easily as I do," James quipped. "These are tough little guys. I doubt they'll even look at you funny."

He gave her a quick once-over, then followed with a lopsided grin. "Well, maybe a *little* funny. I'll get you a new camp shirt and shorts so you'll have clean clothes. You probably should wash up before we eat, though. You must have rubbed your eyes when your hands were dirty. You look like a raccoon."

"Since animals are my forte, I suppose that's in

character," Megan replied. "I haven't sneezed so much since I brought home a stray kitten and hid it in my bedroom when I was about Roxy's age."

"You're allergic to cats? Hey, me, too."

"And lots of other things, considering all the sneezing you did today. How can you work up here? I'd think all the tree pollen and weeds would finish you off."

"I'm usually pretty careful," James explained. "And a few headaches are a small price to pay for the privilege of helping these kids."

Megan had been studying his expression, had picked up on the poignancy of his tone. "You can't save them all, you know," she said quietly. "All you can do—all any of us can do—is take one day at a time and give it our best. Then we have to let it go."

"That's a lot easier said than done."

"Yes, I know. I've been praying for the wisdom to stop feeling accountable for everybody else's failings for years. I'm still having trouble."

"Praying?" James gave her a contentious look.

"Why not? I need all the help I can get." Megan paused, wondering if she should go on. "Don't you believe in God?"

"Sure. I just can't see where He'd be interested in hearing from me. I learned to handle my own problems a long time ago. I don't need any outside source telling me what to do. I make up my own mind."

"My father feels the same way," Megan said. "I never was able to convince him to trust the Lord."

"So?"

"So, I failed."

James reached over and sympathetically patted the back of her hand. "Hey, like you said, let it go. People do things that disappoint us all the time. It's not your fault. You can't be responsible for their choices."

Yes, I can, she told herself. Logic had nothing to do with her feelings about her parents. Not a day went by that she didn't wonder what she could have done—should have done—to somehow keep her fractured family together. Such thoughts might not be sensible, but that didn't keep them from haunting her.

Chapter Three

While Megan took a shower in the girls' dorm and got herself spruced up for supper, Roxy helped Inez in the kitchen and James supervised his resident campers' evening chores. Tonight, he'd assigned them to tidy up the area in front of the dining hall.

Several of the boys weren't thrilled to be outside at all, let alone doing yard work, but when James led by example they all pitched in. It was hard to keep any kid interested in a task for long, and he was glad to have genuine outdoor projects for them to do. Learning to work together and respect authority was crucial for their rehabilitation. So was receiving praise when it was due.

"Super job, Mark," he called. "Now give the rake to Bobby Joe and let him finish up all the way to the big tree. Kyle, those dead branches go in the wheelbarrow. That's right. Great."

James let his thoughts drift to Megan as he worked, and he found himself picturing her in surprising detail. Her hair and eyes were dark, like his, but that was where the similarity ended. He already sported a summer tan. She had skin so fair, it would surely burn after only a few hours under the clear Ozark sky. And she was so small that any kid older than nine or ten was probably going to laugh at her if she made any attempt at discipline. The woman was a hard worker, true, but she didn't look as if she could handle a good-sized dog, let alone a horse.

He gritted his teeth. It had been ages since he'd thought about how much he hated horses. The first time he'd seen one up close had been when his parents had sent him to military academy at the age of thirteen. His initial experience in horsemanship had been so traumatic it had left him with a broken arm and a deep-seated loathing of the stupid beasts.

Even before his arm had healed, he'd been assigned to help clean the stalls in the horse barn, which was apparently his instructor's way of pushing him to face his childish fear. Instead, that impossible task had been the equivalent of aversion therapy. If he never touched another horse for the rest of his life it would be fine with him. Two weeks of having one in camp was going to feel like two years.

One of the boys squealed, pointing at the door to the women's dorm. "Here she comes!"

The youngest pair, John and Robbie, began jumping up and down hollering, "Yeah!"

James smiled. Megan was wearing the official Camp Refuge T-shirt and shorts. She'd apparently picked the largest of the shirts he'd laid out for her and it was way too big. That, combined with her wet, slicked-back hair, made her look about Roxy's age. Or younger. If didn't know better, he'd doubt she was even old enough to be out of high school, let alone a grad student.

"Okay," James shouted, gesturing to the boys with a sweep of his arm. "Everybody line up over here with me and I'll introduce you. You, too, Bobby Joe. That's good enough for now. You can finish raking later."

When the youngster hesitated instead of obeying, a wiry, older boy grabbed the rake handle. A tugging, screaming match ensued.

"Zac! Bobby Joe! Knock it off."

James pushed the two apart. They immediately dove at each other. He grabbed them both by the back of the waistband of their jeans to keep them separated.

Zac, whose reach was longer, took immediate advantage. Before James could stop him, he swung his whole body, fist first, and hit Bobby Joe in the face. The little blond urchin let out an ear-splitting wail that sounded powerful enough to shake leaves off the trees.

Letting Zac go, James lifted Bobby Joe higher to protect him from further injury. Blood was already dripping from the child's freckled nose and trickling down his face. The minute the boy saw blood on his hands and realized he'd been injured, he began to sob.

Megan hurried to join the group, greeting everyone with a cheery "Hi, guys!" in spite of the racket. Her eyes widened when she saw Bobby Joe. "Ooh. What happened?"

"It's a long story," James said. "Aaron's busy in the office. Watch the other boys for me while I take care of this, will you?"

"Sure."

As James walked away, she smiled at the remaining youngsters. They didn't look so bad. A little withdrawn, maybe, but certainly not malicious. Wanting to initiate a conversation and also demonstrate how open-minded she was,

Megan asked lightly, "So, who threw the first punch?"

No one answered. Moreover, all but one of the boys looked away.

"What's your name?" Megan asked him.

The slightly built teen leered at her, then raised his eyebrows and gave her a blatant once-over. "Zac," he drawled. "What's yours, sweet thing?"

Megan managed to stifle her surprise enough to answer, "You may all call me Miss Megan or Miss White," then switched her concentration to the others to avoid further eye contact with the outspoken boy.

"My sister and I've been invited to eat with you tonight," she told the group. "If you'll lead the way, I'd like to see the dining hall."

"Can't," Zac announced. "We gotta wash up first or the old man'll have our hide. Don't worry. I'll take care of it." He then rounded up the smaller boys as if he were their scoutmaster and herded them toward their dorm.

It had occurred to Megan that James might expect her to accompany them but she decided that that much close observation wasn't necessary. Or wise. The boys were just taking a short detour on their way to supper. Besides, she didn't want to give Zac another opportunity to taunt her until she'd learned more about his background. *Sweet thing, indeed!*

She wandered in the general direction everyone else had gone, still chuckling about Zac's ridiculous remarks. Imagine, calling James Harris an old man! If there was ever a guy who *didn't* look or act old, it was the camp director. Then again, he had to be eight or ten years her senior. Making him maybe midthirties.

Which was far from ancient, Megan mused, although right at the moment, her overworked muscles were insisting *she* was at least ninety…and counting.

She rubbed her sore back through the T-shirt. Dressing everyone alike had its advantages, though she would have preferred a color brighter than sky-blue. Oh, well, at least she was clean. The jeans she'd worn during their refurbishing project were so filthy she couldn't have tolerated them much longer.

A melding of wonderful aromas identified the camp kitchen. Looking for her sister, Megan peered through the screen door before opening it. Inside, a middle-aged, obviously harried woman with bright red hair was dashing back and forth between the stove and dining area. Roxy was nowhere to be seen.

"Grab my biscuits out of the oven, will you?" the woman hollered as soon as she spotted Megan. "There's a hot pad over there, on the counter."

"Sure. By the way, I'm Megan White, Roxy's sister. Is she around?"

"In the bathroom primpin', last I saw her."

"That figures. You must be Inez Gogerty."

"In the flesh," the older woman said. "Forgot my manners for a minute there. Sorry. I got behind when the boss showed up needin' ice."

"For the little boy's nose? How is he?"

"Fine. Mostly hurt his pride, I 'spect. That kind of thing happens all the time 'round here. You'll get used to it."

"I'm hoping it won't happen as often after I get my project going."

"The critters? Yeah, I heard. Ol' James's not exactly tickled pink about that. Course, I 'spect you know that."

Megan smiled. "He did mention it."

"I'll just bet he did." Inez looked her over and chortled. "You must be a lot tougher than you look."

"I have my moments," Megan answered. "Have you known Mr. Harris a long time?"

"Since he was knee-high to a grasshopper."

"What was he like?"

"Oh, he was okay." The cook scooped hot biscuits into a bowl, covered it, then handed it to Megan. "That goes next to the green beans. I hope everybody gets here before the fried chicken gets cold."

"The boys are on their way," Megan said. "Zac took them to wash up first."

Inez nodded, her short, henna curls bobbing. "That should be interesting. You want to know what James was like as a boy, you just look at that there Zachary."

"Oh, my."

"Yup. He was a little smart aleck all right. Good-hearted, though, in spite of all the fixes he got himself into. His folks gave up tryin' to cope with him and packed him off to boarding school just in time to avoid a set-to with the law. Nobody heard from him for years. When he finally showed up back in Serenity, he was all growed up."

"Are his parents still around?"

"Nope. Whole family left town after they sent him away. Far as I know, he lost touch with everybody, even his brothers. Course, that wasn't no accident."

Megan was appalled. "You mean, he doesn't want to find them? Why not? They're his family."

"He told me *they'd* disowned *him,* not the other

way around. That's good enough for me," Inez said flatly. "Just because somebody's born into a family doesn't mean they have to stay in it if they're not wanted."

"Don't you think they're worried about him?"

From behind her a deep voice said, "No."

Startled, Megan whirled. James was standing in the doorway, a clean-faced Bobby Joe half-hidden behind him. She forced a smile. "Hi. We were just talking about you."

"So I gathered."

"I wasn't being nosy," Megan explained. "I just wanted to understand what motivates you, what makes you the person you are."

"Hard knocks," he said. "Any other questions?"

"Only why you choose to hold a grudge and cut yourself off from your family," she blurted, before taking time to fully censor her thoughts.

James huffed. "It wasn't my decision to go away in the first place, and it wasn't me who didn't leave a forwarding address. If my folks don't care, why should I?"

"How about your brothers?" Megan asked. "Have you done a search on the Internet? I'll be bringing a laptop with me when I move in. You're welcome to borrow it if you want."

"Believe it or not, Camp Refuge not only has

electricity, a telephone and indoor plumbing, it also has its own computer system. Your notion of us being dumb, backward hillbillies is outdated, Ms. White."

"I didn't mean anything like that. I was just trying to make a sensible suggestion."

"I know." He spoke with resignation and a quiet sigh. "That's a big part of our problem. You're determined to help me in spite of everything I've told you, and I don't need or want any help. It's as simple as that."

"I'd hardly call my work simple," she countered. "You may not take this project seriously, but I do. I don't care how long it takes. I'm going to convince you I'm right and you're wrong." In the background, Megan heard the cook's quick intake of breath.

James, however, began to laugh and shake his head. "I don't suppose it's occurred to you that we might both be a little right, has it? No, I didn't think so." He glanced past her into the dining hall. "Where are the rest of the boys? Did you leave them with Aaron?"

"No. Zac took them to wash up," Megan said. The moment the words were out of her mouth and she saw the look of disbelief on James's face, she knew she'd made a mistake.

"*What?* I told you to watch them."

"You don't have to raise your voice. They're fine. They just went to wash their hands, that's all."

"You'd better hope that's all."

Stomping past her on his way out the front door, James was mumbling to himself. Megan couldn't make out most of what he was saying but she did manage to catch a word or two. That was plenty.

Chagrined, she looked around the kitchen for something to keep her busy till he got back. "Can I help you with anything else?" she asked Inez.

"Nope. Everything's ready. Why don't you take Bobby Joe into the dining room?"

"What a wonderful idea." Megan crouched down to be on the child's eye level and asked, "How about it? I don't know how you do things around here. Will you show me?"

To her delight, the fair-haired boy nodded.

Straightening, Megan took his hand. "Good. Let's start with where we're supposed to sit to eat, shall we? I want to be ready when Mr. Harris comes back."

"Zac hit me," Bobby Joe said.

"I know. That was too bad. You look fine now, though."

"I bleeded on my shirt," he announced, sounding proud. "Bunches. It was gross."

"I saw. Why were you fighting with Zac?"

"'Cause he's mean. I hate him."

"That's too bad. Well, maybe you'll get to go home soon and you won't have to see him anymore."

"Uh-uh."

Megan suddenly realized she'd gotten so caught up in their conversation, she'd spoken out of turn. To glean the most from her project, she knew she'd have to rely on facts, not supposition. Like James Harris, some of the children she'd be working with would never be welcomed at home—if they even had a home. Perhaps Bobby Joe was one of those.

Rather than make things worse, she tried to change the subject by pointing to one of the long tables. "So, do we sit here?"

"Yeah." He clambered onto the bench and folded his hands while Megan joined him. Then he said, "Zac gave me a swirly yesterday."

"A what?"

"He dunked me. My hair got all wet."

"Oh." Megan was starting to relax till the child added, "Yeah. Then he flushed."

By the time James returned with the other five boys plus Aaron and Roxy, Megan had had time to imagine lots of scenarios, most of them bad. She breathed a sigh of relief. Clearly, her previous work hadn't prepared her for the challenges she was going to encounter here.

She glanced down at the angelic little boy seated beside her and smiled. He was a doll, the kind of well-behaved, eager-to-please child who brought out her maternal instincts and made her want to protect him. Too bad the would-be hood who had clobbered him hadn't had the same kind of good upbringing.

The other boys marched up to the table and quickly took their places while Roxy flirted with Aaron in the background.

James remained standing and glared down at Megan. "Don't you *ever* do that again."

"Do what?"

"Leave the boys unsupervised. When I tell you to watch them, I mean *watch* them."

She got to her feet to face him on more equal ground. "Oh, come on. They were just washing their hands. Zac said he'd take care of the littler ones, and it looks to me like he did a fine job."

"That's not the point. You didn't follow orders."

"I'm sorry, okay. I guess I wasn't thinking."

"You can say that again."

"You don't have to yell at me."

"I'm not yelling."

"Well, you sure could have fooled me."

Inez was entering the room, bearing a platter heaped with crispy fried chicken. Megan let her pass, then grabbed James's arm and tugged him toward the kitchen. When he resisted, she scowled. "Come with me. I want to settle this in private. It won't take long."

He gave in reluctantly and followed her through the door. "It better not."

Megan whirled, her voice husky, her eyes blazing. "Don't you dare threaten me."

"I wasn't. I didn't." James gestured back toward the dining room. "What do you have to say to me that couldn't be said just as easily in there?"

"Plenty."

She couldn't believe he didn't realize what he'd done, what he was still doing by not lowering his voice and confronting her as quietly as possible, so she set an example by rasping at him in a near whisper, "You told me not to question your authority in front of the kids, yet you just made me look like a fool in front of those boys—and my sister."

"I did not."

"You most certainly did," Megan insisted. "Everybody makes mistakes. Even me. I was joking when I told you I thought I was perfect. From now on, if you have anything derogatory to say to me, I'll expect you to say it in private."

One eyebrow arched. He gave a slight shrug and spoke more softly. "All right. I'll spell it out for you. These kids may look angelic but many of them are seriously disturbed. One at a time they're usually pretty agreeable. In a group, anything can happen—and often does."

"You mean I'm supposed to treat them like they're in jail?"

"Not exactly. When one of them merits trust we give it, up to a point. Next time you're not sure whether or not to permit something, ask me or Aaron about it first and we'll avoid problems like this."

"That sounds reasonable enough." Megan chanced a slight smile. "I'm sorry I caused you extra worry. I thought my decision to let Zac take them to wash up was perfectly logical."

"I know. It's partly my fault, too. I should have warned you these kids would try to bamboozle you big-time. You've learned that on your own, I take it."

"No kidding. Talk about a trial by fire."

"Everything turned out okay. We'll forget it ever happened. Now, let's go eat before the kids get so hungry we have a mutiny on our hands." He pushed open the swinging door between the kitchen and dining room and held it politely. "After you."

To Megan, the most amazing thing was his apparently complete change of mood. In the blink of an eye, James Harris had gone from delivering angry retorts to being a gracious host. She frowned at him as she passed, unsure if she was reading him right. While her stomach was still tied in knots and her hands were trembling from their encounter, he seemed calm, totally in control.

Everyone stared at them as they left the kitchen together. James headed for his normal spot at the head of the table, escorting her as he went.

Megan slid into the place where she'd been sitting, directly to James's right, because it was the only available space. There was no gracious way to move away from him as she had on the porch. Therefore, she figured she'd better follow his example and start acting more normal or the boys might get the idea they could pit them against each other again.

Seated beside Aaron and Roxy at the opposite end of the long table, Inez quietly bowed her head. Megan was expecting someone to say a blessing on their meal but no one spoke. They simply observed a quiet moment while she used the time to pull herself together.

When everyone suddenly looked up and began talking, she felt much better, much more at ease. She decided to break her silence and let James know she'd simmered down by asking him a question. "You don't say grace?"

"Can't. Separation of church and state," he said. "The silent prayer was Inez's idea. So far, nobody's questioned us about it. Most folks are pretty tolerant out here in the sticks. It's when the kids go home that we may hear complaints."

"I see." Megan lowered her voice for privacy, though she wasn't too worried about being overheard above the boisterous conversation going on at the table. "Speaking of home, tell me about Bobby Joe. What's his situation?"

"He's temporary, like all the others. I'll give you access to our files as soon as you set up your computer."

"What about Zac? Why do you let him pick on Bobby Joe so much?"

James chuckled. "*Let* him? Not hardly. I do my best to keep them apart. Being brothers, they naturally gravitate to each other."

"Brothers?" Megan was flabbergasted. "Those two are related? They're not a bit alike."

"Lots of siblings aren't," he said, offering her the platter of chicken before taking any for himself. "My brothers are far different than I am."

"Oh? How so?"

Passing the mashed potatoes and picking up the bowl of green beans, he spooned some onto his plate. "They were always perfect saints. Sons to make their parents proud."

"And you weren't?"

James chuckled. "According to my folks I was the exact opposite. I got tired of not being able to live up to their ideals, gave up trying and let them think what they wanted."

"I'll bet they'd be proud of your work here."

"I don't care one way or the other. It's enough to know I'm doing the right thing. I don't need validation from them or anyone else."

Nodding, Megan sighed. At the far end of the table, her sister was carrying on an animated conversation with Aaron Barnes, leaning close and fawning over him. The poor guy was blushing, obviously embarrassed by all the extra attention.

Megan shared the young man's discomfort. Though she felt sorry for James because of his estrangement from his family, there were times, like now, when she wished she didn't have to worry about anyone but herself, either. To make matters worse, James was also watching the young people. Judging by the look of consternation on his face, he wasn't any happier about their interaction than she was.

Softly, Megan said, "I'll take care of that as soon as Roxy and I are alone. She'll back off. I promise."

James, who had been taking a sip of ice water as she spoke, looked incredulous, burst into laughter and promptly choked.

Megan slapped him on the back. "Serves you right. It wasn't *that* funny."

"Yes, it was," he managed, while coughing into his napkin. "I can just picture that little sisterly talk."

"I'll expect you to speak to your helper about it, too," Megan added. "We can't put all the burden of good behavior on my sister."

James coughed again, finally getting his irritated throat under control. When he lowered the napkin he was grinning like he'd just heard the best joke of his life and was still chortling over the punch line.

"Okay," Megan said, "what's so amusing?"

"You are. Anybody who thinks she can convince a fifteen-year-old girl to stop making eyes at a good-looking college boy is out of her ever-lovin' mind."

Chapter Four

The remainder of the meal passed rapidly for Megan. She took part in the boys' lively discussions as much as possible, hoping to gain insight into each of their characters, while trying to keep an eye on her sister, as well.

By the end of the evening she had decided that all but the two littlest boys were better actors than most Academy Award winners—and those two were strong runners-up. Listening to them chatter, observing their innocent expressions, she would never have guessed that their short lives had been filled with enough trauma and adversity to overwhelm most adults.

Megan didn't realize how exhausted she was, both mentally and physically, until the evening meal and kitchen cleanup had ended. If James hadn't followed her out onto the porch, expressed a desire to speak with her in private and asked her to wait there while he located Aaron and turned his charges over to him, she would have loaded her flirtatious sister into the truck and headed straight home.

Regrettably, she'd been so bumfuzzled by James's surprising request, she hadn't been able to come up with one single plausible excuse to leave immediately.

Instead, she'd simply nodded and said, "Okay. I haven't seen Roxy in the past few minutes, either. I imagine when you find your helper, you'll find her, too. Tell her I'm about ready to go, will you?"

"Sure."

She plunked down on a comfortable-looking padded glider and gave it a push with her feet. Fireflies flashed pale green as they rose randomly from the forest floor, making nearby bushes look as if they were decorated with twinkle lights. Frogs along the river started to croak.

Enthralled by the aura of peace, Megan yawned and fought to stay alert. If James didn't join her soon, the smooth back-and-forth swinging was liable to put her to sleep. It prompted memories of the old glider where she and Roxy had often met to share secrets and giggle over silly nothings when they were girls.

Poor Roxy. Where was she going to choose to live when these two weeks were over? Megan didn't want to interfere in her sister's choices, she simply wanted everyone in their family to get along. Was that too much to ask?

Senses lulled, she sighed and closed her eyes.

James's softly spoken "Are you asleep?" made her jump.

Her eyes flew open. "Oh! You startled me."

"Sorry."

He joined her on the glider just as he had on the porch of the old cabin, apparently not aware of her desire to keep her distance.

Trying to inch away without making a big deal of it, Megan scooted left as far as possible and folded her arms across her chest. "It's okay. I was just resting my eyes."

"Since you weren't snoring, I'll buy that excuse." He concentrated on the way she was rubbing her upper arms with her hands. "Are you cold? I can loan you a jacket if you want. It gets kind of chilly when the sun goes down."

"I have a jacket in the truck if I need one. I'm fine. Really. Just a few goose bumps." *Probably caused more by sitting out here with you than by air temperature.* "Did you find my sister?"

"Uh-huh. I left her with Aaron and the boys so you and I could talk. They're all watching a kids' movie."

"That sounds safe enough." She hid another yawn behind her hand.

"I didn't mean to keep you up past your bedtime. Are you sure you'll be okay driving home? It's a long way to Little Rock."

"Actually, I only have to drive as far as Bald Knob, but thanks for asking. It's not the time on the clock that's getting to me, it's the effort we put out today. You're a tough guy to keep up with when you set your mind to finishing something."

"I could say the same for you. Neither one of us would have had to work so hard if you'd been reasonable about taking another cabin, you know."

"Give it a rest, Harris. My aches and pains are well worth it. That cabin is perfect."

"Okay. So, what else will you need? Besides decent furniture, I mean."

"Well, right now I could use a big bottle of horse liniment." She chuckled at the silly look on his face. "Just kidding. Actually, I'm looking forward to buying some pretty curtains, maybe bringing a few things from home, too. If you can provide a couple of beds and a dresser, I think I can come up with the rest."

"Will cots do?"

"Minus the mice, sure." Megan grinned at him. "I don't think I could get Roxy to sleep there if she thought we were still knee-deep in vermin."

He made a face. "It wasn't that bad. Besides, you're the one who insisted on living in a barn."

"Storage shed, but never mind. Just do the best you can. I'll cope."

"I was planning on giving you a brand-new frame and mattress. I think I can come up with a second one for your sister."

"Thanks."

"You're welcome."

With a deep, relaxing sigh, he planted his feet and gave the swing an extrafirm push, then said, "I wanted to talk to you alone because I wanted to tell you what a good job you did this evening. The boys like you."

"I like them, too. They're an interesting bunch. I'm looking forward to reading their files."

"How soon will you need the furniture?"

"Before Monday, if you can manage it."

"I think I can. I still need to run safety checks on the plumbing and wiring. And I want to make sure the space between the rafters and the ceiling isn't full of surprises, like wasp nests. Once that's done, you'll be free to take possession."

"Sounds great." Megan got to her feet and faced him. "Well, was that all you wanted?"

"No." He joined her, stepped closer, then stopped as she edged away. Looking contrite, he jammed his hands into his pockets. "Actually, I want to apologize, too."

"What for?" She managed to maintain a respectable distance by continuing to back up, even though her thumping heart insisted she was still far too close to him.

"Pick a reason."

Megan placed a finger against her cheek and struck a pose as if thinking. "Wow. So many choices. Where should I begin?"

"You could start with my general attitude," he said, half smiling.

"Good choice!"

"You don't have to rub it in."

"Okay. Apology accepted."

"Thanks. Look, I realize I was out of line when I reprimanded you in front of the boys. I'll probably make other mistakes, too. If I do, I'll keep saying I'm sorry. But I don't apologize for taking my job seriously—for taking these *kids* seriously. I'm all they've got."

Megan found herself smiling at him as if he were a lovable but none-too-bright pup instead of an educated colleague.

"Not anymore, you're not," she countered. "Now, they've got me, too."

Unusually alert during the long drive home, Megan assumed that her fatigue was simply on hold and waiting to take over as soon as Roxy was through chattering about Aaron Barnes. If that ever happened.

"He's so handsome," Roxy crooned. "Don't you think so?"

Megan pretended ignorance. "Who?"

"Aaron, of course. Who'd you think I meant?"

"Well, you did start out the day by admiring Mr. Harris. Remember?"

"That old guy? Eesh. What a pill."

Laughing, Megan shook her head. "Old? You're the second person who's called him that today. I hardly think he's all that ancient, honey."

"For you, maybe." Roxy made a face. "I'd rather kiss a frog."

"Who said anything about *kissing?*"

"Hey! You're blushing," Roxy said. "Don't tell me you're finally interested in romance! Oh, wow. I thought I'd never see this."

Megan gripped the steering wheel tighter and composed herself before answering. "Mr. Harris and I are professional associates, that's all. I admire the work he's doing. It takes a special person to face troubled kids every day and not give up." She paused, then added, "I was probably blushing because I was picturing you kissing Aaron. If that idea has even crossed your mind, I want you to promise me right now you won't get involved with him. He's much too old for you."

Roxy giggled and slid down in the seat so she could prop her bare feet on the dash.

"Roxanne? Promise me."

"Too late," the teenager said with pride. "He's already kissed me." Another giggle. "And it was wonderful!"

Roxy had dozed off on Megan's couch as soon as her head hit the pillow. Sleep didn't come nearly as quickly and effortlessly to Megan.

Thinking too much was the biggest part of her problem, she reasoned, yet how could a person whose mind was whirling like an Arkansas tornado turn off those thoughts enough to relax? Consciously trying to do so was obviously the wrong approach. So was employing logic—assuming she possessed any anymore.

She stared at the ceiling of her bedroom, wondering how she was going to continue to help her sister, and do her job, without destroying the peace of the camp.

Would prayer help? Undoubtedly. Of course, that was taking for granted that she had the mental ability to concentrate on her heavenly Father while most of her brain felt like it was getting one of Bobby Joe's swirlies!

Picturing such a silly scenario brought a chuckle. She rubbed her eyes. Clearly, this project at Camp Refuge had cast her as a student, as well as a teacher. She could show the children how to properly care for animals and encourage love and trust between them, but the real results were going to be up to God—on all fronts.

Megan could understand how easy it would be to adopt James's habit of seeing himself in charge of whatever happened, good or bad. However, there was much more going on here than that. It looked as if she was about to enter another advanced course in what she'd come to think of as "God School."

Self-doubt immediately began to flutter at the fringes of her mind like tiny moths circling a lightbulb on a summer's eve. How could she hope to show anyone else the path to peace and happiness when she, herself, lacked absolute trust? She was human. She had misgivings, fears. Everybody did. The question was, why was she still fretting about those concerns when she should have given them over to the Lord's keeping and gone to sleep long ago?

Megan took her frustrations out on her feather pillow by pounding it into a more comfortable shape.

Something told her she'd just been given her first exam in the new class God had enrolled her in. And she'd flunked, big-time.

James awoke to daylight from a fitful sleep, wondering how any time could have passed. If he hadn't had his boys to worry about, he'd have pulled the covers over his head and dozed for at least another hour. Unfortunately, he could hear that they were already up so he had no choice but to join them.

He got to the door of the communal bathroom in time to see Zac put a headlock on his brother and start for one of the stalls.

James's loud "Good morning" put a quick end to the prank.

"Hey, Mr. Harris," the oldest boy called, giving Bobby Joe a parting pat on the head, "long time no see. I thought you were gonna sleep all day."

Yawning, James raked his fingers through his hair to comb it back. "Don't tempt me."

Zac was grinning and leering at the same time. "You sure stayed up late enough last night. So, when's that sweet thing comin' back to see us?"

The arch of James's eyebrow was no accident. He stared at Zac without speaking until the boy flinched, then looking around, James said, "I expect you all to treat Ms. White with the same respect and consideration you give me and everybody else who works here. The same goes for her animals. Understand?"

As soon as the boys nodded, he continued. "When she gets here and sets up her program, I'll make up a daily schedule. Anybody who wants to learn about the animals will have a turn. But…if any of you cause trouble, that will end your chances to spend time in her campsite. Is that clear?"

Mumbled answers of "Yes, sir" echoed in the cavernous, tiled bathroom.

"Good," James said. "I'm glad to hear it. Now, if you guys are finished with your showers, I'd like to take one."

All the children scattered except Zac, who lounged with his thin back against a porcelain sink, crossed his arms and grinned from ear to ear.

James eyed him cautiously. "Yes?"

"I was just thinkin'," Zac drawled. "If you want me to keep those kids busy so you can romance Miss Megan without bein' disturbed, it's gonna cost you."

"Oh, it is, huh?" His mouth twitched with a suppressed smile. "And what makes you think I have any such notion?"

The boy huffed. "Man, if you don't, you're dumber than I thought you were."

It was all James could do to keep from bursting out laughing. Instead, he grabbed a towel by one corner, flicked it in the boy's direction with a snap that purposely fell short of making a connection and roared "Out! Out!"

Zac broke and ran, leaving James shaking his head and chuckling. What a kid. A real character. Smart, all right, but as unpredictable as Ozark weather.

Thinking about the boys in his care, James turned on the shower the same way he always did, stripped and stepped under the spray. The first few moments were fairly comfortable. Then the water turned icy!

Roaring, James dodged and groped for the hot water faucet. It was already on full force. Could those kids have used up all the hot water? Nothing like that had ever happened before. Shivering, he gave the taps a quick twist to end his torture and stared at the plumbing.

Now that the water had ceased to flow he could hear the buzz and titter of young voices outside the bathroom door. He listened closely. It sounded like they were laughing. And Zac was loudest of all. Had they set him up? Rigged the shower? Probably, but how?

His teeth chattering, James grabbed a clean towel and dried himself vigorously to bring back some warmth. Zac again. It figured. If that kid ever got himself squared away in society he'd probably do well in whatever career he chose. The trick was going to be in convincing him to choose lawful endeavors. Concepts of right and wrong were hard to explain to kids who had never been taught there was any difference.

James snorted derisively, thinking about life in general and his boys in particular, as he dressed. Making the right choices could be hard for adults, too. He ought to know. He'd struggled with the same fundamental principles of good versus evil for a lot longer than he wanted to admit. If it hadn't been for a teacher who had cared what happened to him and intervened on his behalf, there was no telling what he might have eventually done with his life.

Continuing that example of caring and concern was a big component of his journey into a career of service. It was going to be a long time—if ever—before he'd feel he'd adequately repaid the enormous debt he owed Ralph Clarkson.

And speaking of owing—if his suspicions proved true, he owed Zac plenty.

Instead of putting on his shoes and socks, James walked barefoot and silent to the closed bathroom door. He listened. There was a soft scuffling and tittering on the opposite side of that door, further convincing him that his icy shower had been no accident.

Slowly, cautiously, he closed his hand over the knob, then jerked the door open without a word.

Bobby Joe and Mark tumbled into the room. The others managed to keep their balance and immediately scattered, squealing and shouting.

James righted the two boys, released Mark and concentrated on Bobby Joe. "Where's your brother?"

The blond-headed child's lower lip was quivering. "Over—over there," he whispered, pointing toward the laundry room.

"Okay. Now shush," James said, placing his index finger across his lips. "Stay right here."

It wasn't hard for James to approach the laundry area without being heard. He paused at the open door and peered past the washing machines. There was Zac, kneeling at the base of the water heater and fiddling with the valve on the line that fed the boys' dorm.

James paused long enough to stop grinning, then stepped into view with a gruff "Hey! What're you doing?"

The boy sprang to attention. "Um, nothin'. Nothin' at all. I was just—"

"Save it," James countered. "I know what you did."

"You do?"

"Sure. You heard me holler and you wanted to make sure the water heater was working right, so you came in here to check on it for me. That's right, isn't it?"

"Ummm…if you say so."

Half of James's repressed smile returned in spite of his determination to play out the scene seriously. "Would you say it's working now?"

The boy backed away with a shrug of his thin shoulders. "Beats me. I don't know nothin' about plumbing."

"Well, I do. And it looks to me like that valve is only partly open. Maybe that's why I ran out of hot water in the shower this morning."

Another shrug. "Maybe."

As he bent to check the water heater, James said, "Just so you'll know, in case this problem comes up again, if you shut off the intake instead of the outflow, you can run the holding tank dry and maybe burn out the heating element. If that happened, by accident of course, we'd all be taking cold showers." His voice lowered. "Understand?"

"Hey, why tell me? I don't have nothin' to do with keeping this dump running."

"No, but I do." James stood and laid a hand on the boy's bony shoulder. "The next time you think something needs fixing around here, I want you to come tell me, not take matters into your own hands. Okay?"

"Okay. Sure. No sweat."

Shepherding Zac out of the laundry room and back to the dorm, James was thankful the prank hadn't caused any lasting damage. He knew he should reprimand the boy, but no real harm had been done. There would undoubtedly be plenty of other instances when Zac would need his wings clipped. James figured he'd save any show of serious displeasure for a more important infraction.

Besides, he mused, there was no way a kid as sharp as that really believed he'd gotten away with the prank. He knew full well the camp director was on to him. And he also knew James had accepted being given a cold shower. It was all part of the unofficial game they played while feeling each other out, trying to find a common ground without having to give in too much.

James knew the game well. He'd played it for years on the side of the underdog. Now that he was the authority figure, he didn't want to lord it over the boys. He'd decided long ago that the best way to prove he deserved respect was to earn it by being fair rather than insisting on absolute obedience. All the rules, all the threats in the world weren't going to make a kid like Zac behave for long unless he truly wanted to. There was a very fine line between being the boy's mentor and his jailer. That was the line James intended to walk.

Chapter Five

When Megan arrived back at Camp Refuge she was pulling a loaded stock trailer.

She parked by the cabin, helped Roxy move the rabbit hutches into the shade so the animals wouldn't be stressed by the heat, then headed down the hill to report their arrival to James.

He almost flattened her when he threw open the door of the main hall and burst out.

Off balance, Megan staggered back at the edge of the top step, arms windmilling. "Ahhhh!"

"Oops." James caught her neatly. Steadied her. "Sorry. I thought I heard somebody drive in. I was on my way to see if it was you."

"It's me, all right." She straightened, disengaged his hold and smoothed her shirt over her clean jeans. "I just wanted you to know we'd arrived."

"Have you looked at the cabin yet?"

"Not closely. Why?"

"No reason."

His expression was hard for Megan to interpret. One moment he looked smug and the next almost embarrassed. The swing from enigmatic to endearing unsettled her almost as much as his brief but necessary touch had.

She gave him a nervous smile. "What did you do—rig it so I'd get a bucket of water dumped on my head when I opened the door or something?"

"Me?" He made an obvious pretense of wounded feelings. "I assure you, I never play practical jokes, Ms. White."

Megan hesitated an instant, then said, "Okay. Sorry. It shouldn't take me long to get my animals settled in. You can bring the kids up later, after lunch, and I'll give them an idea of what I'll expect when they work with me."

"You mean *if,* don't you?"

Disappointment colored her response. "My mistake. I'd forgotten you were so dead set against my project."

"Hey, I didn't say that."

"You most certainly did."

She knew the best thing to do was leave him before she gave in to the urge to blurt out something she'd be sorry for. Considering the way she was feeling at the moment, it wouldn't be long. Besides, keeping company with James when she didn't have to was bound to give Roxy more erroneous ideas about their nonexistent relationship. That was the *last* thing she wanted.

Megan stood proud. "If you'll excuse me, I have work to do. I don't want to leave my animals in the trailer any longer than necessary."

Whirling, she clomped down the steps and crossed the dirt lane that passed for a road inside the campground. If James Harris thought he could thwart her by keeping those kids away, he had another think coming. Nobody was going to stop her. Nobody. She was in the right and she was *not* going to back down. The gall of that man. "*If* they choose to come see me! Ha!"

Increasing animosity gave her feet wings as she climbed the hill to her cabin. She didn't care what he'd done to the place in her absence, what kind of awful furniture he'd dug up for her. She was not quitting. Not if she and Roxy had to sleep on the floor and store their clothes in cardboard boxes!

Megan's jaw was firmly clenched, her lips pressed into a thin line as she breezed past her surprised sister. She grabbed the knob, threw open the door to the cabin—and froze. Her heart sank. Her breath caught. Oh, dear! It was worse than she'd thought. Much worse.

James had not only given her the things she'd asked for, he'd added so many other amenities, the place already looked like a warm, welcoming home. There was a settee, complete with throw pillows, a reclining chair beside a combination end table and magazine rack, a small dinette set with two matching chairs, and regular twin beds instead of the cots she'd expected.

This was *awful!* She'd practically spit in his eye just now, assuming he'd tried to sabotage her comfort, when he'd actually done the opposite.

Sadly, there was only one thing to do, and the sooner the better. It was time for another apology. A humongous one. And this time, it had to come from her.

Roxanne had trailed her into the room. "Oh, wow! I can't believe the difference."

"Neither can I."

"So what's your problem? You look like you just ate a bug or something."

"No, but I am about to have to go back down the hill and eat my words. Buckets hasn't shed all her winter coat yet but she's a tough little mare. She'll be fine waiting in the trailer till I get back.

So will Beethoven. But move Rocky's cage into the house for me, will you? And let Wiggles go with you so he can sniff around and make himself at home. Just keep him on a leash for now."

The teenager gave a snort of disgust. "Anything else? Want me to put up the big corrals by myself, too, while I'm at it?"

Megan chose to avoid an argument by overlooking the sarcasm in the girl's voice.

"No, thanks. We can do that together as soon as I get back. I don't expect to be gone for more than a few minutes. It doesn't take long to eat crow." She pulled a wry face. "I just hope all those feathers don't get stuck in my throat while I'm trying to swallow my pride, too."

Megan found James in the main hall, supervising the boys. Some of them were studying while the others worked on craft projects that reminded her of activities in a normal summer camp. Flat wooden sticks, colored paper scraps and dots of white that looked suspiciously like glue littered the floor.

He smiled and started toward her as soon as he realized she'd come back. "Hi. How was the cabin?"

"It's wonderful," she said quietly. "Thank you."

"You're welcome."

The younger boys had followed him and crowded around to offer their own greetings. Megan would have preferred to speak to James alone, but since they had an audience she figured she owed it to him to confess in the presence of the children. After all, what better way to teach than by good example?

She put a finger to her lips to shush their eager babbling, smiled and led everyone over to the homework table where the older boys, Zac and Mark, were still seated.

"Everybody please listen for a second, okay? I came to tell you I'll be ready to show you my animals soon."

As soon as the chorus of "Yeahs" subsided, she continued. "And I also came to apologize to Mr. Harris."

Serious, subdued, she turned to James. "I'm sorry I misjudged you. You fixed up my cabin much better than I deserve, especially after the way I spoke to you. I truly am sorry."

James gave her a lopsided smile. "Apology accepted. Actually, it wasn't entirely my idea. Inez made a few suggestions and the boys and I did the work."

"Yeah!" Bobby Joe piped up. "I helped."

"Me, too! Me, too!" Kyle echoed.

Megan was even more touched. She crouched and opened her arms to them. "How sweet of you all. Thank you."

To her chagrin, none of the youngsters accepted her offer of a group hug. Even the littlest ones, Robbie and John, held back.

She quickly straightened and pretended nothing unusual had occurred. Clearly, these children were not used to displaying affection—or receiving it. They were like the hospitalized babies she'd read about. Ones who were given daily massages gained weight much more rapidly than expected and were ready to be discharged a lot earlier than others. Loving touch made all the difference. Sadly, when children were not cuddled as babies, they often had trouble forming interpersonal relationships for the rest of their lives.

That kind of emotional damage was one of the things she hoped to overcome with her companion animal study. Yet it was much more than that. Megan wasn't sure exactly when the change in her focus had taken place but she knew her work had long ago ceased to be a simple scholarly study. Her heart and mind were now so intertwined with what she was doing, it was impossible to separate herself from her goals. Which was probably why she'd taken James's negative opinions so to heart.

Looking into his eyes, she sensed a depth of understanding beyond what she'd expected. He hadn't missed the importance of what she'd learned when the children had held back, nor was he condemning her for trying to embrace them. He seemed almost appreciative of her efforts, though clearly not surprised at the rebuff.

Megan smiled slightly and nodded at him. "Well, I've disturbed you enough. I hope you can find the time to bring everybody up to my camp later."

"What time?" he asked.

"Around three? That should give us time to set everything up."

"Do you need any help? Aaron isn't here today but I can have Inez watch the boys if you need me."

"I appreciate your offer but we can handle it. Roxy and I loaded the horse panels ourselves. They're not heavy. Just cumbersome."

"Okay. Then three o'clock, it is," James said. "We're looking forward to it. Aren't we, gang?"

Another chorus of children's shouts punctuated his statement.

Megan reached out and laid her hand lightly on

his arm to reinforce her parting words. "Thanks. And again, I'm really sorry I misjudged you."

"No problem."

The muscles she felt beneath his warm skin twitched. He pulled away abruptly.

Comparing his reaction to what she'd just experienced with the children, Megan blinked. New possibilities nibbled at the fringes of her imagination. Was James Harris good at his job because of his formal education? Or did he understand the children in his care so well because he was like them?

Her heart instantly went out to the stoic man. Perhaps there were adult emotional walls as well as youthful ones that needed breaking down at Camp Refuge.

If that were the case, she was up to the challenge. She had to be. The good Lord would not have placed her here if He hadn't been sure she was capable of accomplishing whatever He asked of her.

Feeling positive and in control of the situation, Megan bid everyone a polite goodbye and started back for her cabin.

By the time she was halfway up the hill, however, she'd begun to question her conclusions. Her fingers still tingled from where they'd brushed his bare forearm, and her pulse was far too rapid to have been boosted into orbit by the easy climb to her camp. Therefore, she had to be reacting in a personal way to being around James Harris again.

Okay, fine. She could accept that. So he happened to affect her sympathies the same way a wounded or mistreated animal did. So what? That didn't mean she had to behave any differently toward him than she would toward the children she'd come to help.

And it certainly didn't mean Roxy had been right when she'd envisioned a budding romance between them. No, sir.

It was normal to feel love for her parents, her sister, her pastor and innumerable fellow Christians—men, women and children—so why not share the same brotherly affection with someone like James?

In theory, that sounded perfectly plausible to Megan. In practice, however, she wasn't sure she was going to be able to pull it off without getting too involved. There was something very special about the camp supervisor. Something compelling she couldn't quite put her finger on. Something that struck her as the kind of attraction that might prove dangerous to her own peace of mind—if she let down her guard for an instant.

* * *

It was well after three o'clock before Megan saw James leading his charges up the hill. When she'd learned that Aaron wasn't currently in residence, Roxy had retired to the cabin to read a romance novel, which left Megan alone to greet her visitors.

She ordered her mottled gray Australian shepherd to heel, then called out a pleasant, "Hi. I was beginning to worry you might have changed your mind."

James didn't smile. "We were delayed."

"Why?"

"There was another fight."

"What about?"

"Do you really want to know?"

"Of course I do." Megan scowled.

"Okay. Mark and Kyle were arguing over who'd get to ride the horse. I don't know who threw the first punch but by the time we were through, I was almost ready to cancel this afternoon's visit."

"You can't blame me for that."

"If I did, we wouldn't be here now," James said flatly. "Any disturbance in our daily routine can have the same kind of upsetting effect. That's one of the things I've been trying to explain to you."

"Then your so-called routine is too rigid," she countered. "Kids need to have fun."

"There's reassurance in sameness."

"Balance is better." Glancing at the overly subdued boys who were still standing in line behind him like baby ducks trailing their mother, she lowered her voice to ask, "Precisely what makes you think otherwise, Mr. Harris?"

"Besides my time in the school of hard knocks, you mean?" He made a soft sound of derision. "I have a master's in education. Will that do?"

"I wasn't questioning your abilities. I was just trying to figure out what makes you tick."

"I don't tick. Neither does Camp Refuge. It hums like a well-oiled machine. At least it did until recently."

Megan wasn't about to let him get away with a remark like that. She grinned. "Oh? Well, you know what happens to even the most expensive engine if you never change the oil. It grinds itself to death. And I think your oil needs changing, mister. You're starting to grind something awful."

The resulting look on his face was so comical she had to giggle. Some of the boys began to chuckle, too. At her side, the spotted shepherd wagged his gray stub of a tail so vigorously his whole body shook, yet somehow held his place by her side as she'd instructed.

She laid a steadying hand on the dog's head. "Good boy, Wiggles. Stay."

The boys looked as eager to make the dog's acquaintance as he was to make theirs. Megan smiled broadly. "Does everybody here like dogs?"

Each child nodded in turn as she singled him out and waited for an answer. Satisfied, she said, "In that case, I'd like you to meet Mr. Wiggles. He loves everybody so you don't need to worry about anything but his kisses. Ready?"

Greeted by a unanimous chorus of "Yeah!" she released the dog with a hand signal and a joyful "Okay," watching in delight as he bounded up to the group of children and was immediately surrounded. There was certainly no reluctance to reach out and embrace the four-legged ambassador of unconditional acceptance, was there?

Megan was filled with delight and appreciation for the direction her life had taken. If, after her parents' divorce, she'd chosen to go live with her strict father the way Roxy had, there was no telling what would have become of her or where she'd be now. Maybe she'd have rebelled, too.

No, I wouldn't have, Megan told herself with calm assurance. God had had a wonderful plan for her all along. Even as a teen she'd glimpsed inklings of it.

She wouldn't break the rules and try to proselytize the young people she'd be working with, but there was no way she could live her daily life without relying on faith. Her actions were her real sermon.

And speaking of actions, it looked as if the boys were beginning to tire of dodging dog kisses and trying to pet Wiggles when he wouldn't hold still.

"Okay," she said, moving past James to the children. "Let's start with a simple rule. This is important. Listen up, guys. You, too, Wiggles."

She waited until all eyes were on her, including the dog's. "I don't want you coming up here and playing with the animals unless you're invited. Not even if Mr. Wiggles looks lonely and treats you like his best buddy."

Zac's sly grin gave her pause so she stared straight at him and added, "I don't care how many excuses you can think up. I mean what I said. Got that?"

"Yeah, yeah," the thin teen muttered.

"Good. I wouldn't want everybody to lose the privilege of having fun just because one of you broke the rules. Any questions so far?"

"Yeah," Zac drawled. "How come your dog's got one brown eye and one blue one? He looks real weird."

"He's an Australian shepherd," Megan said. "Lots of them have unusual eye color. It's just how they're made. The same goes for his tail, in case you haven't noticed."

"What tail?" Bobby Joe asked with a puzzled look. He leaned to peer at the dog's rear end. So did Mark.

Megan smiled. "Exactly. Most dogs do have tails. But Aussies are usually born without them. It doesn't bother Wiggles a bit. We can still tell when he's happy because he wags his invisible tail so hard his whole body…wiggles."

She waited for the snickering to die down, then said, "Okay, now that everybody has met my mean old watchdog, let's go see my horse, Buckets. Follow me."

Megan started toward the pens, her dog obediently trotting at heel on her left. The boys came along in a loose group, bouncing, skipping and jabbering excitedly. The only child who wasn't acting his age was Zac.

He hustled his walk to match her stride. "That's a dumb name for a horse."

"Oh, I don't know. When I first got her, Buckets didn't even have a regular name. She'd been starved till she could hardly stand up anymore. I started calling her Buckets because every time I saw her she had her nose stuck in a bucket of feed."

"If she was so bad off, how come you took her?"

"Because she needed a friend. And I needed a horse like her. By the time I'd nursed her back to health we were good buddies."

"Horses don't know stuff like that, do they?"

"I'll let you make up your own mind after you've taken care of Buckets for a little while. I think you'll be surprised."

Zac snorted derisively. "Yeah, sure."

Megan noticed that although the boys had gathered outside the nearest railing of the horse pen, James was hanging back. Was he looking for errors in the way she kept the children safe? Perhaps. It didn't really matter. At the moment, she had six boys to educate about the proper way to approach a horse, while keeping said horse from mistaking their fingers for snacks.

She brought out a cube of sugar to demonstrate. "Now watch what I do so you'll know how to give her treats. First, look at Buckets. See how her eyes are on the sides of her head instead of in front, like ours? That's so she can see on both sides at the same time and stay safe from predators."

"Like mountain lions?" Bobby Joe asked, awed.

"If there were any left in Arkansas, yes." She looked to James. "Are there?"

"Not according to Game and Fish."

"That's a relief." Megan smiled. "I'm sure Buckets is glad, too."

She paused, held her hand perfectly flat, palm up, and bent to show the boys. "Always offer food like this. When you get close, Buckets can't see what's right in front of her nose. If something smells good, she'll nibble at it to see if it tastes good, too. She's not being mean, she's just confused. If your fingers are in the way, they can get tasted before she realizes it's you she's biting."

"Eeew," Zac said. "Finger food."

Megan had to work to keep from laughing. "Right. That's why it's best to always present a treat on a flat palm." She reached into her pocket. "I have plenty of sugar cubes. Who wants to go first?"

No one came forward. A mere fourteen hands tall, Buckets wasn't big for a full-grown horse but Megan knew the mare would appear impressive viewed from the perspective of a child. All they'd need was one boy brave enough to feed her and the others would line up to do the same.

Megan demonstrated how gently the mare lipped the treat off her palm, then looked at Zac. "How about you?"

He raised both hands in front of him and backed away. "Not me, lady. I don't want no horse spit all over me."

"Her nose tickles."

"Uh-uh. No way." Safely distant, he shoved his hands into his pockets and shook his head insistently.

Megan could see that none of the others were willing to step forward when their eldest peer had set such a strong negative example.

"Okay," she said, smiling. "No problem. Let's have Mr. Harris do it first to show you how easy it is."

If she had looked at James's face before speaking, she wouldn't have tried to draft him. A person didn't need a degree in psychology to see that the man was displeased to have been included in her presentation. Well, it was too late to do anything about that now. He'd have to grin and bear it.

Megan motioned with her whole arm. "Come on. Show the boys there's nothing to be afraid of."

He came, all right, looking as if his best friend had abandoned him, his favorite truck had been wrecked, he'd just eaten a meal of unripe wild persimmons and had been punched in the stomach for dessert. Clearly he was having to force himself to approach. If it hadn't been for the boys watching his every move, Megan doubted she'd have been able to talk him into helping at all.

"Offer the sugar on your open hand," she said. "Then hold real still and she'll take it from you."

The private look James shot her way as she handed him the sugar cube was anything but amiable. It was a good thing Buckets cared more about food than anything else, including how friendly her benefactors might be, Megan thought, because if she'd been in the horse's shoes, she might have nipped a man with such a rotten attitude, just on general principles!

Chapter Six

Megan couldn't believe the man's absurd reluctance. What a shame he didn't prize the affection animals offered. In respect to their immense tolerance, they were often like abused children who looked to their abusers for solace because they knew no alternative.

The young people at Camp Refuge were not the only ones who needed to learn how to enjoy and fully appreciate the blessings of God's creations, were they? A certain stubborn man could use a dose of the same medicine.

Megan smiled, amused at the picture those thoughts created. She could see herself holding a big spoon brimming with the antidote for James's paradoxical disposition and trying to coax him into opening his mouth to take it.

"Spooning it in won't be the hardest part," she muttered. "Getting him to *swallow* will be the real trick."

He jerked his hand away before Buckets could gobble up the sugar. "What?"

"Nothing. Sorry." Realizing she'd been thinking aloud, Megan blushed. "Tell you what. This is taking longer than I'd planned. Let's leave Buckets and go see something smaller. I think you'll all like Rocky."

The abject relief on James's face almost made her laugh. Poor guy. He'd been about as eager to feed the horse as she would have been to offer one of her pet bunnies to a hungry snake. She didn't care if it was the way of nature for creature to eat creature, she didn't intend to facilitate it. Which was one reason she'd chosen not to include reptiles in her menagerie. Besides, they weren't exactly cuddly.

On the other hand, studies had proven the beneficial physical affects of petting an animal's warm, soft fur. Not only did doing that have the advantage of encouraging a feeling of rapport and companionship, it also lowered a person's blood pressure and slowed his or her pulse.

Megan knew from personal experience that there was wonderful solace to be found in having a pet. When it seemed no one else understood her feelings, her animals were always empathetic. They might not fathom the depths of her needs but they gave all they had, which was good enough for her.

Little Rocky was an instant hit with everyone. James had to smile at the flying squirrel's antics—and at its owner's. Over her camp uniform, Megan had donned a loose shirt with big pockets. Rocky was playing hide-and-seek by scampering over her shoulders and ducking in and out of those pockets.

Just when it looked like the tiny squirrel would finally hold still, it took off again, made a mad dash up to Megan's shoulder and hid under her hair, bringing a chorus of squeals and laughter from the boys.

She giggled, too. "Hey, that tickles."

"He never runs away?" James asked.

"Hasn't so far. I've had him four years and he's never made a break for it. I think he sees me as his private tree." She blushed. "Until I learned to wear something loose that he could crawl into easily, some of my demonstrations got kind of interesting."

Chuckling, James nodded. "I can imagine. He

sure likes to hide. I guess he's cute. It's hard to tell exactly what he looks like when he's moving so fast."

She reached back and gently cupped the tiny animal in her hands, bringing him forward and letting him peek out between her fingers.

"Rocky," she said, bending so the boys could get a good look at him, "I'd like you to meet my new friends."

Seeing flying squirrels from a distance had never given James a clear picture of how cartoon-like the species actually was. Rocky's big black eyes were oversized for his little face and his rounded ears were far larger in proportion to his head than those of a mouse. If there ever was a creature that embodied sweet innocence and natural appeal, it was that squirrel.

"His fur is very silky," Megan said. "You can all take turns petting him if you do it slowly and don't make too much noise. We don't want to scare him, do we?"

"No, ma'am," Bobby Joe said, obviously in awe of both Megan and her pet.

James stood back till all the boys had had a chance to touch the finely striped fur. He hadn't intended to take part in Megan's exhibition but when she held the little squirrel up to him, he stuck out a forefinger and acquiesced. The cinnamon-brown coat was so thick, so fine, short and soft, it felt more like warm velvet than the fur of an animal.

"Very nice," James said, doing his best to ignore the knowing look on her face.

"I'm glad you like Rocky better than poor Buckets. Someday, you'll have to fill me in on why you're not crazy about horses," Megan murmured for his ears only.

"In your dreams," James countered. He watched her tuck the now-weary Rocky into her pocket and button the flap. "Are you going to introduce the boys to the rest of your menagerie now?"

"If you have no objections."

He shrugged nonchalantly. "None at all."

"Do you have anything against burros?"

"Cousins of horses? Count me out."

"They're really cute, big ears and everything."

James arched an eyebrow. "And a big mouth, judging by the sound of that braying. Folks can probably hear him all the way to Serenity. Does he holler like that all the time?"

"No. Only when he's feeling left out. Soon as we're done and I put him in with Buckets for company he'll quiet right down."

"I sure hope so."

Dropping back, James brought up the rear as Megan led the boys around her cabin to where the burro was penned. As he'd suspected, it was one of those tattered-looking, dusty-gray animals with a darker stripe down its spine and across its withers. It had ears the size of canoe paddles. When it lifted its head to bray, it laid those enormous ears back against its neck and, sides heaving, put its whole body into the effort. It sounded more like "haw-hee" than "hee-haw." The boys started imitating the sound, adding to the cacophony.

Gathering the children closer, Megan spoke softly so they'd have to be quiet to hear her. "This is Beethoven. I call him that because he's so musical. I'll bring him out and you can all pet him at the same time if you want. He won't mind. He's used to a lot of attention. He really likes people."

James arched his eyebrows and rolled his eyes.

"Of course, he's also very stubborn sometimes. Maybe we should name him Mr. Harris, instead of Beethoven."

"Oh, no," James said before the joke could go any further. "Having two of us with the same name would be way too confusing. Besides, I never sing."

"Never?"

The mischievous twinkle in her eyes nearly

made him smile in spite of his resolve to remain solemn. "Never."

"Not even in church?"

"Nope. My Sundays are spoken for. I don't get out much."

"You can't work 24/7!"

"Oh? Why not?"

"Because it's inhuman. It's un-American. It's—"

"It's what I want," he insisted. "This job is my life. I chose it. I like things the way they are."

"I never said you didn't."

"You implied I shouldn't be so dedicated." Folding his arms across his chest he faced her, waiting for an argument.

Instead, Megan snapped a rope on the burro's halter and led it out of its small pen, pausing just beyond the gate. She scratched Beethoven's fuzzy forehead and let the children get absorbed in petting him before she spoke aside to James.

Her voice was gentle, her manner subdued. "What I was trying to point out was everyone's need for rest, for downtime. That's all. I know what it's like to be so gung ho that you work yourself to death. I did that in college. Believe me, total immersion in my studies was more than counterproductive. It was unhealthy."

"You made yourself sick?"

"In a manner of speaking." She paused. "I had an emotional breakdown."

He sensed how difficult that admission had been for her and softened his stance. "I'm sorry."

"Don't be." Megan shook her head slowly, as if entertaining the sweetest of memories. "I'm not. I had to get all the way to rock bottom before I gave in enough for the Lord to get my attention and lift me up. The trip was rough but worth it, believe me."

"I'm not going to even pretend I understand what you just said."

"That's okay," Megan said with a laugh. "You'll have two whole weeks to figure it out."

By evening, Megan was exhausted. After making the drive up from Bald Knob, getting her animals unloaded and safely settled, introducing the boys to the project and unpacking her clothes and personal items, she was so tired she regretfully declined James's invitation for supper.

"Thanks," she said, yawning behind her hand. "Roxy wants to join you but I'll take a rain check. I'd probably doze off at the table and fall headfirst into my mashed potatoes."

"That would liven up the meal."

"Yeah. I'll bet the kids would love it."

James chuckled. "I can guarantee they would."

Megan leaned on the edge of the half-open door to her cabin. "I'm afraid I'm done for the day, in more ways than one. Tell the boys I'll see them tomorrow."

"They'll be disappointed."

"They'll also learn that adults have lives beyond working all the time, unlike somebody I could mention."

"I work hard because I enjoy it," James countered.

"I know. And I admire your dedication. You're doing a marvelous job."

"Do you really think so?"

"I wouldn't have said it if I didn't mean it."

He smiled. "No, I don't suppose you would. Thanks."

"You're welcome." Another yawn slipped out.

"Hey, I'm keeping you when you should be relaxing." He backed away from the door. "Have a good night."

"Thanks. You, too."

She watched him turn and descend the wooden steps, then start down the hill toward the dining hall. There was still a spring in his step. She, on the other hand, felt like an old washrag, wrung out and limp.

Pushing her hair back off her forehead she noticed it felt damp. Little wonder. The humidity so near the Spring River had to be close to a hundred percent. Thankfully, there was also a slight breeze filtering through the trees. The warm evening would have been stifling without it.

Megan couldn't recall the last time she'd been so tired she'd lost her appetite. Till now, she hadn't realized what a toll the long day had taken. Not only had she been worried about her darling animals—and her sister—she'd felt as if she were on display and being tested every moment James Harris was nearby.

"That's because I was," she murmured. No wonder she was worn-out.

She sat down in the recliner, leaned back and sighed. A cooling draft from the open window soothed her. Outside, a whippoorwill called. Another answered. Tiny tree frogs began a squeaky chorus, punctuated by the louder croaks of others of their species.

Her mind drifted. Reality faded. Soon, sleep took her back in time. She and her sister were seated on the lawn in front of their childhood home. They were picking broad spears of grass, holding them taut between their thumbs, and trying to blow over them to make them whistle.

"Come live in Calico Rock with Mom and me," Megan said. "It's not too late to change your mind."

Roxanne shook her head as she pulled up another tuft of grass. "No way. Daddy needs me."

"*I* need you. *We* need you," Megan argued. "You act like it's Mom's fault their marriage broke up."

Roxy's eyes flashed. "Well, it certainly isn't Daddy's."

"It is so."

"No way. You're just being hateful."

Megan sighed. "Okay. I didn't want to be the one to tell you this but somebody better. Our father's been doing bad things. Hurting Mom. They had a big fight about it. That's why they're getting a divorce."

"No way!" The younger girl jumped to her feet and started away. "I don't believe you. He didn't do anything bad. He wouldn't."

Following, Megan grabbed her arm to stop her. "You're still a kid. How would you know?"

Roxy whirled, red with anger, and jerked free. "I'm old enough."

"You're a baby. I'm almost eighteen."

"That doesn't make you a genius," she screeched. "You don't know what you're talking about! Daddy loves us. Mom must be crazy to think he doesn't. And you're just as bad as her for believing it."

Megan's eyes grew moist, blurring the scene and leaving her casting around for her sibling through a haze of tears. Poor Roxy had never been able to get past their father's charm and see the man for what he was, had she?

On the other hand, Megan had sided with their brokenhearted mother so completely she'd given their father little opportunity to repent or explain his supposed indiscretions. And that had been the final wedge that had split their family irrevocably.

Half-awake, Megan tried to shout to her sister, to beg her not to go away. Her voice choked with emotion. Her cheeks were wet and flushed. The images in her mind were fading rapidly.

"Wait," she called, "don't go!"

A sense of loss weighed heavily on her heart. She fought awakening. In the distance a dog barked. Wiggles? Growing consciousness brought a return to the present.

Megan's lids fluttered, then lifted. Her eyes snapped open. Someone was bending over and staring at her, practically nose to nose. Only the belated realization that it was James Harris kept her initial gasp from turning into a scream.

"Megan? Megan, are you okay?"

"Of course I am." She rubbed her eyes and brushed the tears from her cheeks. "What are you doing here?"

He pointed to the end table. "Inez sent you a bite to eat. When I got to the porch I thought I heard you crying. I was afraid something was wrong so I came on in. I didn't mean to scare you."

"It was just a bad dream," she alibied. "I'm fine."

"Your sister's reading the boys a bedtime story. Do you want me to stay with you till she gets here?"

Megan pulled a face. "No need. I'll be fine. I always have nightmares when I'm stressed or overtired."

"You're probably hungry," he said.

"I don't think so."

"I do. Skipping meals is bad for you."

She gave him a lopsided smile. "You've been hanging around little kids too much, mister. You're starting to treat everybody like one."

"Only if they deserve it." He lifted one edge of the foil cover from the plate and waved it under her nose. "This is chicken and potato salad. If you're not going to eat it soon, we'd better refrigerate it so it doesn't spoil."

"You could have left it on the porch."

"Why tempt Wiggles? He's out there, remember? The bones might splinter and hurt him. You wouldn't want that to happen, would you?"

"You barge into my house, scare me out of my wits and you're blaming it all on my poor innocent dog?"

"I didn't barge, I knocked. You were too busy fighting dragons to hear me so I did the only sensible thing. The screen door wasn't latched and the door was standing wide-open. If you're afraid of prowlers you sure have a funny way of showing it."

"I'm not afraid of anything. I just expect a little privacy, that's all." She hadn't meant her words to sound so reproachful. Before she could soften her stance, however, he answered in kind.

"Fine. From now on, even if you're incapacitated, you can either drag yourself down to the mess hall for meals or starve. How's that?"

"Ridiculous," Megan said with a wry smile. "But acceptable. I do appreciate your concern, I'm just not crazy about your methods. My heart's still pounding."

"Then don't get hysterical in your sleep again."

"Humph. I'll make every effort not to. Thanks for caring about me. And thanks for worrying that I'd be hungry. It was sweet of you."

James reared back as if ducking a punch. "Whoa. There you go again, besmirching my character. I'm not sweet. I'm just trying to keep my camp running on an even keel."

"Whatever." The warmer hue of his cheeks amused her. "I promise to make every effort to avoid accusing you of being nice again, okay?"

"Especially in public."

"Especially in public."

She watched him edge away, as if he'd suddenly realized their current circumstances were far too private and was uncomfortable about it. That reaction was interesting. It meant he was acknowledging her as a woman, not merely a colleague. It also demonstrated his high morals. If he hadn't cared about giving the wrong impression, he wouldn't have worried about being caught alone with her.

Megan was still smiling about their encounter long after James had left. Whether he liked hearing it or not, he was a real sweet guy. The kind of person who'd make a good, reliable friend. She hoped, before the end of her project, he'd learn to think of her the same way.

Chapter Seven

Roxy moped around for two days, waiting for Aaron's return. When he finally did show up at the camp again he avoided her as if she were contagious, much to Megan's relief. If they actually had exchanged a kiss, as Roxy had claimed, the young man had obviously thought better of it since then and decided to keep his distance. Given his apparent change of attitude toward her sister, Megan saw no reason to go out of her way to mention the possible rule infraction to James.

When he questioned her about Aaron's moodiness, however, she spoke the truth. "Roxy probably made a pass at him and scared him."

James scowled. "What makes you think that?"

"Some things Roxy said. She tends to exaggerate but I suspect she tried to get him to kiss her."

The muttering that followed that statement was too muted to interpret fully but Megan got the gist. "Hey, lighten up," she said. "I've warned her to leave him alone and it looks like Aaron is more than ready to see that she does."

"And that's supposed to make this idiotic arrangement work? If you believe that, you're as crazy as your sister. So, are you going to drive her home or shall I?"

"Nobody's going to drive Roxy anywhere. I promised Mom I'd give her time to think things through by keeping her with me, and I intend to do just that."

"What about the boys? I thought you were supposed to be up here helping them."

"There's no reason why I can't do both."

James shook his head and scowled. "Oh, really? What about Zac?"

"What about him? I thought we were talking about Aaron."

"No," James drawled, "we were talking about your sister. That girl has as many emotional hangups as half the kids the state sends me."

"Nonsense. You're too used to looking for problems. There's nothing wrong with Roxy that a cooling-off period won't fix. She's lived with our dad for five years. He's recently remarried. Once she adjusts to the idea that she's not the only one he loves she'll be fine."

"The only one? What about you? You're his daughter, too, aren't you?"

Megan's lips pressed into a thin line. "When my father and mother divorced, I stayed with Mom. After they split up, I hardly ever saw my dad."

"Then what about your sister? You two are still close, aren't you?"

"I like to think we are," Megan said softly. "I went away to college soon after the breakup. With me in school, even if we'd lived under same roof, Roxy and I wouldn't have seen that much of each other, except on holidays and summer vacations."

"So now you're doing penance."

"I never said anything of the kind!"

"You didn't need to." James sighed quietly. "All right. This is our problem as I see it. Roxy is infatuated with Aaron. He's been avoiding her. Are you with me so far?"

"Yes. So?"

"So, I caught Zac pricking himself with a pin, trying to tattoo the back of his hand with an *R* inside a heart. I checked his file. There's nobody in his life with that initial—except your sister."

"Uh-oh."

"No kidding. I suspect she flirted with Zac to get Aaron's attention and Zac fell for her tricks, hook, line and sinker."

"You can't be sure of that. Roxy may have had nothing to do with how he feels. I can tell she isn't a bit interested in him."

"Can you?"

"Of course. I've always had a sixth sense about things like that. It's similar to the way animals tell friends from enemies. I just seem to know what the people around me are feeling."

"Is that so?"

Megan faced him, hands fisted on her hips, chin high, and declared, "Yes, it certainly is."

"You can even tell how I feel?"

"Within reason, yes."

"Then it won't surprise you if I do this," James said.

Before she realized his intention he'd slipped an arm around her waist, pulled her closer, planted a kiss on her slightly parted lips and abruptly released her.

Breathless, Megan could only stagger backward and stare at him. He looked irritated, though she couldn't imagine why. His short-lived kiss had certainly not been disagreeable. Truth to tell, it had left her so bumfuzzled she could hardly move a muscle, let alone think straight. Her lips still tingled, her arms were covered with goose bumps and she wondered if she was about to land in a dazed heap at his feet.

She only wished he hadn't pushed her away before she'd had a proper chance to either return his surprising show of affection or slap his face. Or both.

"Have I made my point?" he asked gruffly.

Megan shook her head, still in awe of what had just occurred. "Point? What point? I don't have a clue why you did that."

"Then you're less discerning than that oak tree over there," James said. "You may understand animals but you don't have any idea what people are thinking, including your sister. I suggest you keep a close eye on her, Ms. White. That girl is trouble with a capital *T.*"

"You're wrong," Megan argued.

All James said as he turned to leave was, "I sincerely hope I am. For everybody's sake."

The first inkling Megan had that there was another kind of trouble brewing was the arrival of a Fulton County sheriff's car the following afternoon. She'd been letting the boys take turns riding Beethoven bareback while she led him around the yard. Seeing them freeze and stare silently at the black-and-white vehicle, she joined their observation.

When it became clear that the uniformed officer had come alone, the youngest children relaxed. Only Zac remained alert, as if poised to face danger.

Megan touched his arm, making him jump. "I didn't mean to startle you," she said.

"No problem." He was clearly feigning calm.

"There's no reason to be afraid of the police, you know. They protect us."

"I can take care of myself."

"I'm sure you can. So can I. I don't mind getting a little help now and then though."

"Don't need that kinda help," the youth said.

"Not now, maybe. But you should keep an open mind. You may want police assistance someday."

"Not likely."

Having read Zac and Bobby Joe's files, she could understand his point of view. He'd come from a family that had been fractured by crime and the ensuing punishments. No doubt he blamed the authorities for most of his problems, though the real guilt lay with the adult relatives who had tried to use the boys as a cover for their numerous thefts.

Looking back on her own childhood, Megan was chagrined. "Sorry, Lord," she whispered. "I can see I didn't have it so bad. I'm sorry I questioned You."

Zac had been listening. "What?"

"I was just talking to God," she explained. "Thanking Him for the wonderful things in my life."

"Sounds pretty weird to me."

"Not to me. Aren't you thankful for being here with your little brother instead of having to go to separate homes? I hear you two like to stay together."

"Taking care of the kid is my job," Zac said. "I promised."

"Then you and I have something in common. I promised my mother I'd look after Roxy. Roxy's been pretty unhappy lately. Confused, too. But that's understandable. She still has a lot of growing up to do."

The boy grinned. "Looks pretty grown-up to me."

"On the outside, maybe. Inside, she's still my little sister. She always will be, just like Bobby will always be your little brother."

"I guess." Zac averted his gaze. "Do you think she likes me?"

"As a friend? I'm sure she does."

"Yeah, well, I know I'm not all muscles like that Barnes guy but I'll fill out soon. My uncle's real strong. He can beat up anybody. I'm gonna be just like him."

"There's more to success than having big muscles," Megan told him. "Even strong men need to use their brains if they want to succeed. Look what happened to Sampson."

"Who's he? A wrestler?"

"No, he was even stronger." She smiled and shook her head. "The Bible says he pulled a whole building down on top of himself to kill his enemies."

"He croaked, too? That was a pretty stupid move."

"Maybe. The point is, the bad choices he made in the past were why he was in such terrible trouble."

She gave that thought a chance to sink in before she added, "Life still works the same way today. If we don't make a mess of things to start with, there's a lot less to clean up later."

Zac glanced past her and chuckled. Beethoven had decided to relieve himself right in front of her porch. "Speaking of cleaning up," the boy joked, "somebody'd better grab a shovel before that gets tracked into your cabin."

"An excellent idea," she said pleasantly. "You'll find a manure fork in the bed of my truck."

"A *fork?* I ain't fixin' to eat the stuff!"

Laughing, Megan handed him the burro's lead rope. "Here. Hold this while I go get the fork. You'll catch on once I show you how it works."

"I don't know," the teen drawled. "I may be smarter than that guy who knocked a house down on himself but I'm pretty slow when it comes to learning to use farm tools."

James waited until the boys and Aaron were back in their dorm, washing for supper, before he headed up the hill to speak with Megan. She was running fresh water into a big plastic tub in the horse pen when he arrived.

"I'm glad everything went well," he said. "No broken bones…yet."

"I assure you I'm very careful." She wiped her forehead with the back of her hand, trying to keep perspiration from stinging her eyes. "Those kids are a handful."

"Tell me about it."

Megan grinned. "I just did."

"Very funny."

"I thought so." Studying his expression more

closely she sobered. "Hey, what's wrong? You look worried."

"I am. I want you to make sure your door is locked tonight when you go to sleep. And take the dog inside with you so he can warn you if there's a prowler."

"I saw the police car today. Is there a burglar in the area?"

"Something like that."

"Give me all the details. I don't want to become a victim through ignorance. Wiggles can help us patrol the camp, too, if you think it's necessary."

"It shouldn't be. There may not even be a problem, at least not for anybody but Zac and Bobby Joe."

"Why just them?" Her brow furrowed.

"The sheriff got word that their uncle, Ethan Ewing, is out on bail and may plan to come here to get them. All we're supposed to do is keep an eye out and call the cops if we notice anybody strange hanging around."

"That could be too late."

"I know. Unfortunately, we have no choice. I'm not too worried. The man's a known thief, but according to our files he's never been violent."

Megan's eyes widened. "Oh, yeah? How many uncles do the boys have?"

"I don't know. Why?"

"Because Zac told me how much he admired an uncle who used to beat people up just for fun. If that's his uncle Ethan, I think I'd rather skip meeting the guy."

"Can't say I blame you. Just in case there is a connection, either Aaron or I will walk you and your sister to and from the dining hall. I don't want you making the trip alone anymore, especially not after dark."

"And I thought all I had to worry about up here in the hills were ticks and chiggers and snakes."

"Hey! That's a great excuse," James said. "We'll tell your sister and the boys that you saw a snake and you're scared to go walking alone."

"It's the snakes I don't see that bother me," she said wryly. "Especially the big, two-legged kind."

Supper was over and James was putting the boys to bed when Roxy decided she wanted to leave the dining hall and go back to their cabin immediately. Megan suggested they wait for James to return.

"No way. I'm not a baby. And I'm not scared of any old snakes, either. You can hang around here if you want to. I'm going home."

"If you help me wipe down tables, time will

pass before you know it." The set of the girl's jaw told Megan she was wasting her breath. "Okay. I'll go tell Aaron we're ready to go."

"Aaron?" Roxy brightened. "Cool. I thought we had to wait for Mr. Harris."

"Yes and no. James said Aaron will walk us to our cabin any time he's not available himself. But remember what I told you. Aaron is working here. He's not hanging around in order to keep you entertained."

"You don't want me to find somebody special and be happy, do you?"

"Of course I do. Just not yet, okay? You'll have plenty of time for that when you're grown-up."

"Like you? Yeah, right. I'm not going to wait till I'm old and wrinkled to fall in love."

Wrinkled? Megan gave a soft chuckle. The absurd notion of being a has-been at twenty-three tickled her. Amused, she headed for the boys' dorm to fetch Aaron.

Before she got to the porch she could hear the boisterous boys. She knocked on the frame of the screen door. "Hello! Anybody home?"

James appeared immediately. He was frowning. "What're you doing out by yourself? Why isn't Aaron with you?"

"I thought he was over here with you," Megan

said. "Roxy's ready to go back to our cabin. I came to fetch a bodyguard, like you wanted."

"I just sent him back to the dining hall. Didn't you pass him?"

"I don't know. I may have." She scanned the forest through the deepening twilight. "I wasn't expecting to see him. I guess I didn't notice."

"Then I'm doubly glad I insisted you be escorted. The way you wander around with your head in the clouds is asking for trouble."

Megan laughed. "Hey, considering the fact my sister thinks I'm so old I'm already over the hill, I think I'm doing quite well." She started to turn away.

"Where are you going?"

"Back to the kitchen."

"Alone?"

Hands on her hips, she gave him a look of derision. "Well, duh. Of course alone. You have the boys to look after. You certainly can't go off and leave them, can you?"

"No," James said soberly. "Okay. Go. I'll wait right here where I can watch you most of the way. When you get safely back to Inez, flash the porch light on and off a couple of times so I'll know you're okay."

Megan gave in to the urge to tease him. She

stood at attention and gave a snappy salute, followed by "Yes, sir!"

The look of incredulity on his handsome face made her laugh aloud. That he obviously didn't share her good humor added to her amusement.

She didn't mean to belittle his concern, she simply thought he took everything far too seriously. *Especially* himself.

Chapter Eight

Inez was the only person left in the dining hall when Megan arrived and asked, "Where is everybody?"

"Roxy left. I think Aaron took her for a ride on the ATV. You know, that noisy, four-wheel-drive scooter thing they all like to take to the backcountry? I heard the motor start up a second ago."

"Oh, dear."

"I wouldn't worry," the older woman said. "Aaron didn't seem to mind. He looked pretty happy to be goin' off with your sister. I was a tad surprised. I didn't think they were gettin' along all that well."

"I wish they weren't," Megan said. She grabbed Inez's arm and tugged her out the door. "Come with me. If Aaron's not back in the dorm when we get there, you may have to stay and watch the little kids for a few minutes while James and I go looking for the bigger ones."

"Aaron's a good boy," Inez insisted. "I know his family. He'll look after your sister fine."

"I don't doubt that for a minute," Megan said. "But it's dark out there, Roxy's got him all to herself and they're probably riding double on that all-terrain thingie. I'm not worried about her safety. I'm worried about who's going to protect *him*."

They hit the dorm porch just as James was coming out the door.

He scowled at Megan. "You didn't flash the light."

"That's because everything isn't fine," she replied. "I brought Inez along to watch the boys while we're gone."

"Where are we going?"

"Hunting. Grab a flashlight and come on. Roxy and Aaron are out in the woods on your ATV, all by their lonesomes. I don't think that's very wise, do you?"

"No." James matched her strides off the porch and across the dirt road. "How did it happen?"

"All I know is, they were gone when I got back to the kitchen. Inez said they went for a ride."

"Maybe that's all there is to it?"

Megan shot him a look of doubt that was evident even in the sparse light filtering through the trees from the rising moon. "Are we talking about the same two kids we know and love? Get real, Harris."

James had to call Aaron's name twice before there was an answering shout. He pointed his flashlight in that general direction and saw the pair coming toward him. In seconds they'd become a foursome.

Roxy was hanging on to Aaron's arm as if she'd laid claim and was defending her personal property. "We ran out of gas," the girl said with a telling giggle.

James was furious. "What were you doing out there in the first place?"

"Taking Roxy home, just like you told me to," the young man answered. "Miss Megan wasn't in the dining room when we left. Inez said she was with you."

"That's beside the point," James countered.

Aaron shrugged. "What was I supposed to do? I was just following your orders."

"And I wanted to go home," Roxy crooned. "Aaron and I weren't doing anything wrong. Honest."

An Important Message from the Editors of Steeple Hill Books®

Dear Reader,

Because you've chosen to read one of our fine romance novels, we'd like to say "thank you!" And, as a **special** way to thank you, we've selected <u>two more</u> of the books you love so well, **and** a surprise gift to send you — absolutely <u>FREE!</u>

Please enjoy them with our compliments...

Jean Gordon

Editor,
Love Inspired®

EDITOR'S
FREE GIFT
SEAL
THANK YOU

Peel off seal and place inside...

HOW TO VALIDATE YOUR
EDITOR'S FREE GIFT!
"THANK YOU"

1 Peel off the FREE GIFTS SEAL from front cover. Place it in the space provided at right. This automatically entitles you to receive two free books and an exciting surprise gift.

2 Send back this card and you'll get 2 Love Inspired® books. These books have a combined cover price of $9.98 in the U.S. and $11.98 in Canada, but they are yours to keep absolutely FREE!

3 There's no catch. You're under no obligation to buy anything. We charge nothing—ZERO—for your first shipment. And you don't have to make any minimum number of purchases—not even one!

4 We call this line Love Inspired because each month you'll receive books that are filled with joy, faith and traditional values. The stories will lift your spirits and gladden your heart! You'll like the convenience of getting them delivered to your home well before they are in stores. And you'll love our discount prices, too!

5 We hope that after receiving your free books you'll want to remain a subscriber. But the choice is yours—to continue or cancel, anytime at all! So why not take us up on our invitation, with no risk of any kind. You'll be glad you did!

6 And remember. . . just for validating your Editor's Free Gift Offer, we'll send you 2 books and a gift, *ABSOLUTELY FREE!*

YOURS FREE!

We'll send you a fabulous surprise gift absolutely FREE, simply for accepting our no-risk offer!

® and TM are trademarks owned and used by the trademark owner and/or its licensee.

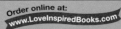

Order online at:
www.LoveInspiredBooks.com

The Editor's "Thank You" Free Gifts Include:

⬤ Two inspirational romance books

⬤ An exciting surprise gift

▶ DETACH AND MAIL CARD TODAY!! ▶

© 1997 STEEPLE HILL BOOKS

JOB 8 (LI-EC-04)

YES!

PLACE
FREE GIFTS
SEAL
HERE

I have placed my Editor's "thank you" Free Gifts seal in the space provided above. Please send me the 2 FREE books and gift for which I qualify. I understand that I am under no obligation to purchase anything further, as explained on the opposite page.

313 IDL DZ3H   113 IDL DZ3G

FIRST NAME   LAST NAME

ADDRESS

APT.#   CITY

STATE/PROV.   ZIP/POSTAL CODE

Thank You!

Offer limited to one per household and not valid to current Love Inspired® subscribers. All orders subject to approval. Credit or debit balances in a customer's account(s) may be offset by any other outstanding balance owed by or to the customer.

Steeple Hill Reader Service™ — Here's How It Works:

Accepting your 2 free books and gift places you under no obligation to buy anything. You may keep the books and gift and return the shipping statement marked "cancel." If you do not cancel, about a month later we will send you 4 additional books and bill you just $4.24 each in the U.S., or $4.74 each in Canada, plus 25¢ shipping & handling per book and applicable taxes if any.* That's the complete price, and — compared to cover prices of $4.99 each in the U.S. and $5.99 each in Canada — it's quite a bargain! You may cancel at any time, but if you choose to continue, every month we'll send you 4 more books, which you may either purchase at the discount price...or return to us and cancel your subscription.

*Terms and prices subject to change without notice. Sales tax applicable in N.Y.
Canadian residents will be charged applicable provincial taxes and GST.

If offer card is missing write to: Steeple Hill Reader Service, 3010 Walden Ave., P.O. Box 1867, Buffalo, NY 14240-1867

BUSINESS REPLY MAIL
FIRST-CLASS MAIL   PERMIT NO. 717-003   BUFFALO, NY

POSTAGE WILL BE PAID BY ADDRESSEE

STEEPLE HILL READER SERVICE
3010 WALDEN AVE
PO BOX 1867
BUFFALO NY 14240-9952

NO POSTAGE
NECESSARY
IF MAILED
IN THE
UNITED STATES

The beam of James's flashlight illuminated the college student's flushed face, making him blink and shade his eyes. Bright pink smudges marked his cheeks and mouth.

"If you were behaving yourself, then you put your lipstick on crooked," James chided. "Or is there some other excuse for that stuff smeared all over you?"

Aaron began to rub his lips with the back of his hand while Roxanne laughed lightly. "I was just thanking him for being so nice."

"Well, from now on, he won't be available to escort you anywhere," James told her. "If you want to go home early, too bad. You'll have to wait till I'm free to take you."

The teenager whined, "That's so not fair."

"I think Mr. Harris is being very fair," Megan countered. "He could have ordered us both out of camp and ended my project. And he'd have had perfect grounds for taking that action, thanks to you. I can't believe you didn't consider those consequences."

"What do I care about you and your old project?" the angry girl shot back. "You never cared about me. You wouldn't have even brought me along if Mom hadn't made you. Why shouldn't I kiss Aaron? At least he thinks about *my* feelings."

"That's enough," James said. "This discussion is over. Aaron, you go back to the dorm and relieve Inez so she can go home. I'll take these ladies the rest of the way to their cabin."

"Yes, sir." The young man had to twist his arm to extricate himself from Roxy's grip. Giving her a small, embarrassed smile, he quickly headed down the hill.

"And you, Ms. White," James said, staring at Roxy, "will not bother my assistant again. He's off-limits to you from now on. If he was a couple of months older, he could be in serious trouble already. Is that clear?"

She sniffed, her chin jutting stubbornly. "Perfectly."

"Good." James turned to Megan. "I know this wasn't directly your fault, but what you told her just now was true. I could end your work here if I wanted to. Tonight."

"I know." Subdued, Megan hoped and prayed he wasn't going to reconsider and send her away after all. "Please don't. I'll keep Roxy with me every minute if I have to. Just give us another chance."

"Agreed. And you remember what I told you about locking your door."

"I will."

"Then let's get you home. It's been a long day."

Megan glanced over at her pouting sister. The girl gave her a look of disdain, whirled and flounced away, headed toward their cabin.

Following, Megan spoke quietly to James as she gestured toward the retreating girl. "Judging by *that,* I'm afraid it's going to be an even longer night. At least for me." She pulled a face. "Guess that's what I get for praying for more patience."

His voice was soft, questioning. "You pray for little things like that?"

"Little?" Megan laughed. "Believe me, James, developing the kind of patience I'm going to need to deal with my sister is no small thing."

To Megan's delight and surprise, Roxy didn't pitch another fit before going to bed. Moreover, by morning the girl was actually acting calm and agreeable. Although Megan was relieved, she kept waiting for the catch. Such an abrupt change of heart for the better was almost too good to be true.

Still, Megan was glad the Lord had answered her prayers for her sister's peace of mind so she could stop worrying and get on with her work. Today, she planned to put Mr. and Mrs. Bunny into an expandable wire enclosure where she could release them on the ground and let several of the boys interact with them while the animals hopped around loose.

Chores had been assigned by capability, meaning Zac had drawn the first cleanup duty in Buckets's and Beethoven's pen. He showed up, accompanied by his brother and Mark, though he didn't seem nearly as eager to be there as the younger ones were.

Megan greeted James as he delivered the boys into her care. "Hello."

"Morning," he said. "Everything okay here?"

"Fine. Better than I'd expected, considering. Did you get your ATV running again?"

"Yes. Funny thing, too. Turned out there was plenty of gas in it."

"What a surprise."

"Yes, isn't it? Well, take care. I'll be back before lunch to pick up these three."

"Okay. Thanks." She turned her attention to the boys and smiled broadly. "Hi, guys. Glad you could come. Are you ready to have some fun?"

Bobby Joe and Mark nodded vigorously. Zac snorted. "You call this fun?"

"I certainly do. The one who cleans the horse pen and brushes Buckets gets to ride her, you know."

"Oh, yeah?" He looked thoughtful. "Okay. I guess I can do that. Just so I don't have to let her lick me."

"You won't. I promise. Let me get the others set up in the rabbit enclosure and then I'll show you what to do."

"Show me? How hard can it be to follow a horse around with a shovel?"

Chuckling, she said, "It won't be necessary to do that, honey. I'm going to put both animals into one pen while you clean the other, then we'll switch them back to the clean one and you can do the second one."

"Two? Hey, nobody said nothin' about doin' two."

"Nobody said *anything,*" Megan corrected.

"That's what I just said."

"Okay. Forget it. You'll find a wheelbarrow around back. Bring it to Buckets's pen. I'll meet you there."

Zac lifted his eyebrows. "Where's foxy Roxy this mornin'? I heard the old man was real fussed at her. What'd you do, lock her up and throw away the key?"

"No. I just reasoned with her," Megan said pleasantly. "On second thought, I'm not sure exactly where she is at the moment, so why don't you wait here with me? I'll hurry. I know you're anxious to start building more muscles."

"Muscles?"

"Sure. Shoveling is great for the biceps and triceps. And if you lift with your legs, too, it'll help your quads."

"Oh, yeah? All right."

And maybe, after you've been with me and my animals a little longer, she mused, *you won't always think of using those muscles to beat up other people.*

It had been hours since her thoughts had returned to the boy's uncle. Chances were nothing would come of the threat he was rumored to pose. Still, it would be foolhardy to ignore the sheriff's sensible warning. If she didn't have Wiggles's judgment and alertness to rely upon, she'd be a lot edgier. That dog had more sense than most humans when it came to telling the good guys from the bad. If danger lurked, Wiggles would tell her.

And speaking of that dog, where had he gone? Glancing up from the youngsters she'd just introduced to the pair of dwarf rabbits, Megan noticed that Zac was no longer in sight, either. Maybe he'd taken Wiggles and gone looking for Roxy. That notion didn't sit too well, considering James's forewarning. If Zac really did have a crush on Roxy, keeping those two apart could be as important as keeping the girl away from Aaron.

Megan instructed her bunny watchers to stay

put inside the pen, then started around the cabin. She was muttering, "Mama, what have you done to me this time?" when she came into full view of the rear yard.

Expecting trouble, she was taken aback by the peaceful scene. Wiggles was lying next to the empty wheelbarrow, his chin on his paws, as if waiting for Zac. Neither Buckets nor Beethoven seemed agitated. On the contrary. The place was *too* quiet. Where was everybody?

"Roxy?" she called. "Zac?"

No answer.

Megan stuck her head in the cabin door. "Roxanne? Where are you?" She was getting concerned. "Roxy?"

Wiggles yipped. He was on his feet now, staring into the thick forest and wagging his nonexistent tail.

"Where'd they go?" Megan asked him. "Out there? Are you sure?"

He barked louder, deeper.

"Oh, brother." She raised her voice and shouted, "Roxanne! You get back here."

No one replied. A chill crept over Megan and skittered up her spine. If Zac was gone, too, maybe Roxy was up to her old tricks, looking for affection anywhere she could find it. Then again, maybe Zac's nefarious uncle had abducted him and taken her sister, too!

"Don't be silly. They're just being dumb kids," Megan told herself.

She scanned the forest. In the past few days the oaks and sycamores had leafed out more fully, almost obliterating the blossoming dogwoods in their midst. If she couldn't spot the bright white flowers that grew so thick among the larger trees, how could she hope to see Roxy or Zac in their muted-blue shorts and camp shirts?

Megan's initial reaction was to forget everything else and plunge into the woods. She couldn't leave the other two boys, of course. She knew that. But, sensible or not, the pull of sibling responsibility and the undercurrent of apprehension were strong.

There was only one rational thing to do. Find James ASAP, tell him what had happened and let him decide what steps to take next. Her mind made up, Megan dashed back around the cabin to end the rabbit encounter.

"Sorry, guys. We have to go. I'll let you and the bunnies play together again later, I promise."

"But…" Bobby Joe started to sniffle and looked ready to cry.

"I need you to do exactly as I say," she ordered. Catching her rabbits, she returned them to the safety of their hutch, then held out a hand to each of the children. "Come on. We're going to go find Mr. Harris. No arguments, okay?"

Flanked by the boys, she hurried down the hill. In the back of her mind, niggling doubt was doing its best to explode into full-blown panic.

Megan hit the porch of the main building at a jog and jerked open the door. Breathing hard, she faced James.

"What happened?" He peered around her at Bobby Joe and Mark. "Where's Zac?"

"Good question."

Grasping her by the shoulders, the camp director held her still to look directly into her eyes. "Explain."

"Simmer down. You're scaring the kids," she rasped, short of breath. "It's not that bad. At least I don't think it is. I just can't seem to find him. Or Roxy."

"What? When did you see them last?"

"Just a few minutes ago. Zac was talking to me while I set up the rabbit enclosure. He sounded like he was looking forward to learning about horses. I can't imagine him just taking off."

"What about your sister? How was she acting?"

"Just fine this morning." She twisted free and

took a step back. "Come on. If we hurry we may be able to find them before they get themselves into too much trouble."

"Unless there's more to it than childish disobedience."

"Like what?"

"You know exactly what I mean." He cast a wary glance at the boys, then looked back at her. "I don't intend to spell it out for you and get everybody all riled up if I don't have to."

"I thought of that, too," Megan admitted. "Do you think there might be a connection?"

"Who knows? Us running around the woods like a couple of idiots won't help anybody, though. Especially not if the person we were warned about is involved. Wait here. I'm calling the sheriff. Then we'll go search your cabin to see if your sister took anything with her."

"But...it might be a false alarm. What if the kids have just gone off together?" She scowled toward Aaron and added, "Like the other night."

"That's almost as bad," James said, visibly upset. "The reputation of my camp is already on shaky ground. If word gets out that we have a breakdown in discipline, it sure won't help."

"Well, you can't blame me for everything. I didn't have any part in the outside threat."

"True. And we don't know whether that's the problem now. I'm just not willing to take the chance it might be. The sooner we get professional help, the sooner we'll have both kids back, safe and sound, no matter what caused them to disappear."

"I hope you're right," Megan said.

James noticed that she was trembling and took her hand, holding it gently, firmly, as he said, "Believe me, I hope so, too."

For once, Megan didn't try to pull away. She knew she needed to draw strength from his touch.

"Lord, help us," she whispered.

Though James didn't comment, she felt his grip tighten as if his hands were adding "Amen."

Then he released her and headed for his office to phone the police.

Chapter Nine

The peace Camp Refuge normally enjoyed soon disappeared in a blaze of flashing lights atop police cruisers and rescue vehicles. Hordes of volunteer searchers gathered in groups to receive their assignments and check their survival gear before starting out.

"I thought you didn't want to draw too much attention to this place. I'd hardly call this keeping a low profile," Megan told James. "Where did all these people come from? I thought Camp Refuge was out in the sticks."

"It is. Serenity is the closest town. It isn't very big for a county seat, but word travels fast around here. Folks care. And they look out for their own. I imagine some of these men came from Hardy, Ash Flat, even Glencoe and

Agnos—and those two places are barely pin-points on the map."

"Amazing. I've seen this level of group concern in my campus church group, of course. It's just kind of surprising to see a whole community joining together this way."

"Why? Did you think only church people cared enough?" He huffed. "Listen, my mom and dad were in church every time the doors opened. On the outside, you'd have thought they were the best parents on earth."

Her voice was tender. "They weren't."

"Not hardly. My mother wasn't so bad, if you didn't mind the way she gossiped and complained about her friends and the pastor behind their backs. It was my dad who was the real prize. He bragged about the important contacts he'd made by belonging to that church, like it was a country club or something. He was real proud of the fact that only the highest class of people were fellow members."

"That's really sad. They missed out on a lot by acting so superior."

"Then you can understand why I don't want anything to do with organized religion."

Megan slowly shook her head. "Sure. But if congregations weren't made up of fallible people, who'd be eligible to go to church? Last time I looked, this earth was real short on genuine saints."

"Except for my parents, you mean."

That made her smile. She patted his arm. "Right. Except for them. Of course, if you choose to hold a grudge, that makes you as unforgiving as they were."

"Let's drop the subject, shall we?" James said flatly. "Right now, we need to be concentrating on locating Zac and your sister."

"I haven't forgotten. Talking about other things helps me unwind. At least it usually does." Looking up at him she said, "I'm really getting scared."

Expecting him to offer platitudes and calm reassurance, she was taken aback when he said, "Yeah. Me, too."

Day turned to night. Frogs croaked and chirped along the slow-moving Spring River. Fireflies were back in abundance and crickets sang their cadence in unison. The moon was nearly full, enabling Megan and the other volunteers to see more details of the territory they were covering.

James had encouraged her to remain with him. While the organized search parties covered the hills in a grid pattern, she followed him to a few out-of-the-way places that the others weren't checking yet. Sadly, there was no sign of the missing teens.

As long as she was busy picking her way through the underbrush and over the rocks with James, Megan's mind was occupied. It was when they rested that she found herself fighting back tears.

"I hate to be such a ninny," she said, swiping at her damp cheeks. "I don't usually cry for no reason."

"I'd hardly call this no reason," he countered. "As soon as you pull yourself together we'll head back. I think you should call your parents, even if the sheriff has already notified them. They deserve to know what's been going on. It'll be easier on them if the report comes from you—especially if it's negative."

"I wish I could oblige," Megan said with a noisy sigh. "Dad's away on his honeymoon with his new wife and her little boy. I don't even know where they went. And Mom's the one who talked me into bringing my sister along. All Roxy wanted was a temporary place to stay. Mom refused to be bothered."

"She'd still want to know, wouldn't she?"

Megan sniffled. "I'm not so sure. I hate to say it, but my parents aren't exactly models of loving perfection, either."

"No kidding?"

Megan raised her hand, palm out, as if taking a vow. "No kidding. See? We have more in common than you thought."

"Dysfunctional families? That's hardly a plus." James shook his head. "However, it does help to explain why we argue so much."

"We do not argue," she insisted, immediately realizing that was precisely what she was doing and seeing the latent humor in it. "Okay, maybe we do argue a little. But it's not like we disagree on everything. I think you're right once in a while."

"Thanks a heap." With a lopsided grin he added, "That's real Christian of you, Ms. White."

"Hey, I give it my best. I'd be much worse if I wasn't a believer…believe me."

"Care to elaborate?"

"Gladly. Take this situation, for instance. If I didn't trust God to bring us through, I'd probably be totally hysterical by now." Her crooked smile mirrored his. "As things stand, I'm saving my screaming and sobbing for later, when I get my hands on my darling sister."

"We'll find them," James promised. "No matter what it takes. I won't give up."

"Me, either."

Growing pensive, Megan studied his compassionate expression, the kindness dwelling deep in his dark eyes. "I happen to believe you and I are sharing this predicament for a reason, James. God knew I'd need a friend like you at a time like this, and here you are."

"That's a pretty complicated interpretation of a simple working relationship," James said. "I doubt I can live up to such lofty ideals."

"By yourself, you can't," she said with a sweet smile. "But whether you like it or not, I think the good Lord is using you. And He never fails."

Weary and dirty, James and Megan returned to the searchers' base camp just before dawn.

James approached the officer on duty at the portable command post. "Any word yet?"

Megan held her breath, dreading the answer. She'd already decided, from the men's overburdened expressions, that no one had found a trace of the missing teens.

"Not yet."

"How much longer will you be here?" James asked him.

"Hard to say. If we don't find any signs of foul play we'll probably pull back pretty soon. No sense using all these expensive resources if there's been no crime."

Megan was appalled. "You can't be serious! What about my sister?"

The man shrugged. "She's a teenage girl. They run away all the time. Usually come home when they cool off, though. Chances are this one will, too, even if she didn't stop to pack her bags when she left. You'll see."

"I can't believe…!"

James took Megan's arm and led her away before she could blurt out more. "Calm down," he cautioned. "Getting mad and yelling at the cops won't help your cause. They're just following normal procedures."

"What procedures? Giving up?"

"No, being rational. You and I are personally involved with the kids. We're naturally uptight. That makes us the worst possible people to boss the job. Let's leave it to the experts, at least as much as we can stand."

Megan's knees felt suddenly wobbly. She sagged against him, glad when his arm slipped around her waist and he pulled her closer.

Resting one hand on his chest she looked up at him. "Oh, James. I feel so inadequate. I want to go right back out and start looking again but I don't think I can stay on my feet much longer."

"You're exhausted. We both are. A few hours'

sleep will do wonders. Why don't I walk you back to your cabin and help you feed your menagerie? Then we'll grab a nap."

Megan's eyes widened. She saw his cheeks redden.

"I wasn't suggesting we nap together," he added quickly.

"I never thought you were. I would like some company while I see to my animals, though. I'm really not ready to be alone."

"I understand."

"You do, don't you?"

Megan put her hand in his as they climbed the hill to her cabin. Funny, she mused. In the past she'd always thought of her four-legged, furry friends as perfect companions, yet she'd just told this man that she'd feel alone if he weren't beside her.

That shift in thinking had caught her off guard. Relying solely on animals for earthly solace had been her answer to adversity for as long as she could remember. So why was she now feeling as if she wanted—no, *needed*—to be with James Harris?

The tension of their current dilemma wasn't enough to explain such a radical change of heart. Neither was the temporary rapport they seemed to have developed while pursuing their mutual goal.

It was more than that. They were beginning to rely upon each other, growing empathetic to the point where they shared their ups and downs without having to always voice specific needs.

Was that what he'd been trying to explain when he'd kissed her so abruptly? Was she just now acknowledging a soul-deep awareness that had been evident to him all along? Perhaps.

Then again, perhaps her imagination was running amok. Stress could do that to a person. Normally levelheaded individuals sometimes did or said absurd things under the pressure of life's trials. Just because she was a Christian didn't mean she'd always recognize the right path when she stumbled across it.

Her human side would see to that.

Rounding the cabin, Megan gasped. Wiggles was panting hard and lying atop the scattered remains of a forty-pound sack of dry dog food. If he'd eaten all the food that was apparently missing, it would swell inside him and he'd soon be in terrible physical distress. It might even prove fatal.

She crouched beside him and commanded, "Roll over."

James joined her. "What's wrong?"

"I don't know if anything is, yet," she said.

Probing the dog's abdomen she looked for the

large, hard mass that overeating dry food would produce. Thankfully, her pet's stomach seemed normal-sized and not tender to the touch.

She rose with a sigh and a shake of her head. "I don't think Wiggles ate too much, so that's good. I can't believe this mess, though. He's never done anything like this before. If I hadn't trusted him to behave while I was gone I wouldn't have left him loose to guard the other animals."

Bending to study the ground, James pointed. "I don't think he's responsible. Look. Raccoon tracks everywhere. I imagine he was busy all night defending his territory. Either that or he made some new friends."

"Terrific."

"I take it he's been vaccinated."

"Of course. For everything."

"Good. Every couple of years we get an outbreak of canine distemper in the raccoon population up here."

"What about the spilled food? Is it ruined?"

"Well, it's up to you, but if he were my dog I wouldn't let him eat it." He gave her a look of mild scorn. "Of course, I'd have been smart enough to keep the open sack in the house, or at least dump the contents into a metal can for safekeeping."

"I didn't want to put it in the cabin and attract more mice."

"So, you got bigger, smarter thieves, instead. What now? Did you bring any spare dog food?"

"No. One sack was supposed to be plenty."

"In that case, we'd better make a run to the feed store in Serenity for more." He held out his hand. "Come on."

"I can't leave. What if they find Roxy and Zac? What if my sister needs me?"

"We'll give my cell phone number to the sheriff and tell him to call us the minute anything turns up."

Still hesitant, she eyed her panting dog. "I can't leave Wiggles, either. Suppose I'm wrong and he starts to get sick? I'd have to rush him to the vet."

"Okay, we'll take him with us. Is that all? Are you out of excuses?"

"I guess so," she said, "unless you'd like to volunteer to go get the dog food for me."

"Can't. If they don't have the same brand I wouldn't know what to substitute."

"That's true. Okay, if you're sure you're not too tired. We could always wait and run errands later."

"I'd rather go while the camp has police protection," James said. "Besides, Serenity's not far."

"Give me a few minutes to clean up and change?"

"Sure. I'll do the same, pass out my number, grab the cell phone and pick you up in fifteen minutes. Will that be enough time?"

"Plenty." As he started to leave she called, "James?"

He paused, turned. "What?"

"Thanks. I don't know my way around this area at all. I really appreciate your help."

"Hey," he said, breaking into a teasing grin, "I'm not doing it for you. I'm doing it for the dog. And I'm buying you a metal trash can with a lid we can fasten tightly."

"You don't need to do that. I can charge everything to the project account."

He laughed. "Not in Serenity, you can't. If you didn't have me to vouch for you, you'd be lucky to get anybody to even accept a university check unless you drove all the way to Wally-world in Ash Flat. Besides, I spent months discouraging the skunks and raccoons from nesting under these old cabins. I don't want them to start seeing Camp Refuge as a free buffet again."

"Okay," Megan said. "But let's take my truck. Wiggles is used to riding in it, and if he gets sick…"

"Enough said," James replied. "Your truck it is. I'll be waiting. Just swing by and pick me up in front of the boys' dorm whenever you're ready."

Smiling, Megan watched him walk away. She felt guilty for agreeing to leave camp while Roxy was still missing, but no good would come of running around wringing her hands and weeping all the time, either.

She closed her eyes. "Oh, Father, please watch over Roxy. Zac, too. Keep them safe and bring them back to us. Please?"

The teardrops she'd just gotten through repudiating slipped over her lower lashes and slid silently down her cheeks. It was a lot easier to quote the verse about rejoicing in suffering than it was to actually live it, wasn't it? She sniffled. No kidding.

If she'd had her choice at that moment, she'd have traded all the patient and unswerving endurance the Bible promised for the knowledge her sister was safe.

"But it's not my decision," she whispered. "So there's no use standing around stewing over it."

Mustering her willpower, Megan splashed water on her face, quickly changed into something she felt was more appropriate for going into town, grabbed her purse and called Wiggles.

He bounded to her and began to wag all over.

"That's right. You get to go," Megan told him. She opened the truck door and affirmed her invitation with a wave of her arm and a pleasant "Okay. Get in."

The dog jumped up and took his usual place on the passenger side of the bench seat, head out the window, tongue lolling. Megan chuckled. By the time they added James Harris to their group, they were going to be pretty crowded. Oh, well. As the driver, she was assured of a comfortable place. James and Wiggles could divide the remaining space however they chose. That, alone, should make this trip interesting.

Heading slowly down the hill, she pulled over in front of the boys' dorm. Many cars and trucks, both official and private, still crowded the narrow dirt lane.

She honked. James came out immediately. He'd spruced up nicely, she noted. Clean jeans and a Western-style sport shirt had given him a rested look that added to his already-considerable charm.

Megan leaned forward to peer out at him past the dog. "Hi. Hope I didn't take too long."

"No. I was just finishing up with the sheriff. He's promised to phone us if anything turns up." As James approached the passenger side of the pickup he began to grin. "I see Wiggles is still okay."

"Yes." She watched the man pause to size up their furry companion and the available space.

"I thought the dog would be riding in the back of the truck," he said.

"Nope. He always rides right there."

"Do you want *me* to get in the back?"

Megan laughed lightly. "Of course not. Just shove him over and climb in. He can sit closer to me."

"Lucky dog," James muttered.

He opened the door and put one foot on the floorboard, rested his hip on the edge of the seat and gave Wiggles a push. Before the dog could recover enough to try to retake the window seat, James was all the way in and had slammed the door.

"Nice move," Megan said.

"Thanks."

"Ready? Got your seat belt on?"

"Almost. I found one end of it but I have no idea where the other end is. I think your dog is sitting on it."

"Reach under him and dig it out. Wiggles won't care. He hasn't bitten anybody for at least a week."

The ridiculous look on James's face when he peeked at her around the dog's ruff made Megan giggle. "Just kidding," she said. "Hang on. I'll help." Giving a hand signal she ordered, "Wiggles. Up."

The dog acted confused but did raise his rear enough to reveal the hidden clasp of the safety belt.

"Got it," James said. "Thanks. I wasn't real eager to go poking around under him. Didn't want to make him mad."

"You've never had any pets, have you?" Megan asked.

"Is it that obvious?"

"Well…"

"My youngest brother had a puppy once. He didn't take good care of it so I started to give it fresh water and stuff. It ran away and I got blamed. That's the closest I've ever gotten to a pet of my own."

"You've missed a lot."

James brushed at the loose dog hair clinging to the left leg of his jeans. "Yeah. I can see that."

Chapter Ten

Serenity was as peaceful and quaint as Megan had remembered. Though she'd only passed through it, she'd been impressed by the old-fashioned atmosphere, especially around the immense brick-and-stone government building in the center of the town square. Except for the presence of a few modern vehicles, the scene could have come straight off a picture postcard from the early 1900s.

"There's a little place on the square," James said. "Bea's Family Café. They serve the best ham and eggs around. Why don't we stop for breakfast while we're in the neighborhood? A good meal will help us get our energy back."

"I don't know.... I don't think we should be away from camp that long."

"Nonsense. We have to eat. And today's oatmeal day up at camp. The way Inez cooks it, it's always lumpy. I don't know about you, but I could use some real food."

"Lumpy, huh? Sounds appetizing." Megan had to admit his description of the café food sounded a lot better than a bowl of oatmeal, with or without lumps. She slowed the truck. "Okay. Where is this place?"

"Right over there," James said, pointing. "You can park across the street by the courthouse so the dog will have plenty of shade."

"Where's the feed store from here?"

"Down the block behind the lumberyard. We can stop there on our way back."

"Okay, if you're positive this won't take too long."

She found a shady parking place, made sure Wiggles was comfortable and still feeling well, then rolled down both windows for ventilation before bidding him goodbye.

Crossing the street beside James she said, "I'll want to go back and check on him every fifteen minutes or so, just in case. He's acting fine, though."

"Except that he seems to be rapidly going bald." He brushed at his jeans again. "At this rate he won't have a hair left by tonight."

Megan smiled. "I know it can seem that way. Actually, he's just shedding his winter coat. It'll get worse before it gets better."

"Wonderful. Maybe you could save it all and knit him a sweater for afterward, in case he's cold."

"Good idea. The color is definitely him."

They were both chuckling when James held the café door for her and ushered her inside. The place reminded Megan of her late grandmother's house in Searcy, thanks mainly to the tantalizing aromas and checkered tablecloths.

Several old men who were seated at the counter glanced at the new arrivals. Their discussion ceased. Three other men and a boy, wearing camouflage hunting overalls and bright orange shirts, looked up from their breakfasts, too. All eyes centered on Megan.

She felt suddenly self-conscious. "Did I forget to comb my hair or something?"

"No. You're fine. They just haven't seen you before. Come on. Let's sit in the back corner so you can do some looking of your own and size everybody else up."

"That'll work. Just so I can watch my truck."

A waitress in blue jeans and a faded T-shirt that said Fulton County Homecoming approached with a steaming glass carafe and a big smile. "Morning, folks. What'll you have? Coffee?"

Megan smiled back. "Yes, please. And your ham and eggs. I understand they're great."

"Comin' up," the middle-aged woman said, filling both their mugs. "You staying at the camp with James, here?"

"Yes."

"Any word on them two missing kids?"

James spoke up. "Not yet. The girl is Megan's sister."

The waitress gave Megan's shoulder a motherly pat. "Well, bless your heart. Don't you worry, hon. My Bert and the whole volunteer fire department's on the job. They'll find her. So, how do you want those eggs? Over easy?"

"Scrambled, please."

Megan marveled at how the woman had offered heartfelt reassurance, then gone right back to business as usual without missing a beat. She wished she had that ability. Rationally speaking, she knew it would be best to continue with her work while she waited for word of Roxy's fate. After all, a lot was riding on the success or failure of her animal therapy project. But how could she concentrate enough to function efficiently when her sister might be suffering?

Suffering? Ha! She's probably just off on a lark, her subconscious countered. *As usual.* Roxy had bucked authority before. Plenty of times. And James had recently chastised her in public for chasing after Aaron. It was likely the teenager had simply pretended to accept her scolding, intending to sneak off and do as she pleased as soon as everyone relaxed. That was far more probable than criminal mischief.

James reached across the table and laid his hand over hers. "What are you thinking about? You're frowning."

"My sister. What else?" Megan said. "I was just trying to talk myself out of being so worried."

"You're overtired. Things will seem better once you've had some rest."

"I don't know. My time at Camp Refuge was too short to start with. I've already fallen behind schedule. I don't want to waste the day sleeping when I should be working with the boys."

"Tell you what," James said. "Give me a copy of your agenda and I'll help you catch up this afternoon, after we've both grabbed a few hours' shut-eye." He smiled wryly. "All except for the horse stuff. I'll leave that to you."

"What is it with you and horses?"

"It's a long story."

She glanced in the direction of the café kitchen. "I seem to have time to listen."

"What makes you think I want to tell you?"

"Humor me. I'm a psych major, remember?

Maybe I can help you get over your unnatural aversion to horses. Wouldn't you like that?"

"No." One eyebrow arched. "I enjoy hating the stupid beasts. I don't even want to think about riding again."

"Again? Now we're getting somewhere. When did you ride before?"

"In military school," he said. "It was not the most wonderful part of my childhood, believe me. I fell off and broke my arm the first time I was ordered to canter. Being the new kid, I was also assigned the nastiest jobs, like cleaning out the stable. That's no picnic with your arm in a cast."

"They made you do that? How horrible!"

Megan's heart went out to the boy he'd been. She recalled Inez comparing him to Zac. If James had been forced to do hard labor in the horse barn in spite of his painful injury, it was little wonder he'd formed such an intense dislike. Logic had nothing to do with gut-level reactions when a conflict was so deep-seated.

"I'm sorry you had such a trying time," she said. "But don't you think it's good for our boys to learn that being around animals can be fun?"

A strange look came over him. "What did you say?"

"Animals can be fun."

"No. Before that. You called them *our boys?*"

"A figure of speech." Blushing, Megan got to her feet. "The air-conditioning in here is making me chilly. I'm going to go check on Wiggles and grab my jacket out of the truck. Be right back."

"Sure. No problem."

James stood politely as she left the table. *Our boys* kept echoing in his head. Every day with Megan held more surprises, didn't it?

He huffed. *Every day? How about every minute. Every second.* The woman was an enigma. Unfortunately, she was getting under his skin to a depth he'd thought impossible. There was something about her that drew him, compelling him to get to know her better, to figure out what made her so different from anyone else he'd ever met. When she'd told him she wanted to learn what made him tick, he hadn't dreamed he'd soon want the same from her.

Through the front window of the café he saw Megan open the truck door and step closer to examine Wiggles. Then she bowed her head and touched foreheads with the subdued dog, exchanging a wordless yet unmistakable empathy.

James marveled. The rapport she had with animals was truly a special gift. There were lots of people who never connected to anyone or anything with that much love and understanding their whole lives.

People like him.

Although he cared deeply for each boy who passed through his camp, he didn't dare let himself get too attached. In order to do his job efficiently he had to remain emotionally distant. That was one of the hardest lessons he'd had to learn, one he was still struggling to master, especially lately.

Zac Ewing's obvious emotional need had hit him like a punch in the stomach the moment the teen had arrived in camp. Seeing the kid's strutting, belligerent manner was like looking into a mirror and viewing himself, twenty years earlier.

James clenched his fists. They had to find Zac and reunite him with Bobby Joe. They just had to. And if Roxy White was in any way responsible for this mess, he was going to see that she was held accountable, no matter how he felt about her big sister.

Still staring out the window, he noticed a jump in his pulse when Megan started back across the street. How *did* he feel about her? He wished he knew. He could count on the fingers of one hand the number of folks who knew details of his dark days in military school, yet he'd opened up and blabbed to her like he had good sense.

At the time, the words had flowed easily. In retrospect, however, James was sorry he'd mentioned any weakness. If he expected to impress her—assuming he ever decided he wanted to—he wasn't going to accomplish it by admitting character flaws.

He rose as she rejoined him. "Is Wiggles okay?"

"Yes. Thanks. He sends you his love." She slid into her chair. "Listen, I just noticed—"

James interrupted. "Before I forget, I need to clear up something. I'm afraid I may have given you the wrong impression. Actually, I liked almost everything about military school. Those teachers toughened me up, prepared me for the job I'm doing now."

"I see." Megan took a tentative sip of her still-steaming coffee. "So, your parents did you a favor by sending you away?"

He stiffened. "I'd hardly go that far."

"You might consider it. I'm not saying their motives were pure or anything. But if you were as wild as Inez told me you were, their drastic decision may have saved you from a far worse fate than a broken arm."

Giving that opinion time to sink in, Megan paused, then went on. "I wish there were a place for my sister like that school. I thought the chance to bring her with me was the answer to my prayers." She swallowed past the lump of emotion constricting her throat. "Apparently I was wrong. I'm sorry she's caused so much trouble. Running away is bad enough. Taking Zac with her is inexcusable."

"Whoa. We don't know what actually happened."

Megan sighed audibly. "I do. Now. That's what I was trying to tell you when I came back from the truck. My jacket is gone. I always keep a windbreaker stashed behind the seat. It's not there now."

"So? Maybe you forgot and left it in the cabin."

"I'll look when we get home, but I don't think so. I think my sister took it."

"What if she did? What difference does that make?" James was on the edge of his chair.

"A lot. It was really hot and humid the morning she and Zac disappeared. Remember? I was perspiring even before I started my chores. If Roxy hadn't been planning on staying out all night, why would she have needed a jacket, especially in weather like that?"

"Good question." He pulled out his cell phone and began to punch in a number. "I'm calling the sheriff. He can check your cabin for us, just in case, and relay the information to his teams if they don't find your jacket. What color was it?"

"Red," she said. "Bright red."

"Good. Should be easy to spot."

Megan's optimism was quickly being replaced by the realization they were no better off than before. As soon as James ended his telephone conversation she said, "I can't make up my mind whether to be relieved or furious."

"Well, the more clues we can come up with that point us away from Ewing, the better."

"I know that's the way I should look at it—and I do. But then we have to lay all the blame on the kids. Especially Roxy. She's the oldest. She should have known better."

James nodded solemnly. "I couldn't have said it better myself."

He fell silent, deep in thought. It wouldn't hurt to let Megan assume that the worst danger had passed, though he knew better. Even without the threat Ethan Ewing posed, there was still the mountain wilderness itself, replete with snakes, biting insects, unstable weather and difficult terrain, not to mention careless hunters. He'd even heard rumors of an occasional amateur moonshiner restoring equipment left over from the 1920s and then defending it violently.

According to news reports there were also occasional drug arrests in remote areas, further tarnishing the reputation of the paradise he loved so dearly. Problems like those weren't exclusive to the Ozarks, of course. They existed everywhere, especially in denser populations. Sheer chance would keep the missing kids safer up here than they would have been, wandering around a big city.

Then again, coping in the backcountry was more a matter of constant awareness than of luck. A savvy, streetwise kid like Zac would be far less likely to get himself into trouble in his home territory. There'd be little or nothing familiar to him in the rocky wilds where he'd gone missing.

James gritted his teeth. The longer Zac and Roxy were out there alone, the greater their chances of meeting with some kind of disaster. They were far from out of the woods—no pun intended—whether Ewing was on their trail or not.

In minutes, James had received a return call telling him the red jacket had not been located.

Megan finished her breakfast quickly, eager to get back to Camp Refuge and search for more clues.

By the time she and James had made their purchases at the feed store and driven home, however, her adrenaline had plummeted and she was more than ready to rest.

She thanked James for unloading the fresh sack of dog food and the new metal can in which to store it.

"You're welcome." He stifled a yawn. "I hate to say this, but if I'm going to help you later I've got to get some shut-eye. Otherwise, my mental processes won't be as good as your squirrel's."

"Rocky's a hard act to follow. He's very smart."

"For a critter with a brain the size of a grape, maybe," James said. "I have high hopes my brain's bigger."

"Undoubtedly. Rocky's little head would never be able to hold all your gray matter."

"Guess I should be thankful for that. I'd hate to hear he was after my job."

Megan chuckled softly. "I wouldn't worry too much. Speaking of your job, don't let me keep you. I know you need to go check on the kids."

"There's no hurry. I called in some extra help so Aaron could give Bobby Joe his undivided attention." He covered another yawn. "Guess I had better go, though. Will you be okay?"

"Sure. I'm fine. Go on home."

"Promise me you'll kick back?"

"With all that noise and confusion down there?" Megan gestured at the group of vehicles still parked around the main buildings, then smiled slightly. "Truthfully, I'll probably doze off the minute I sit down. Tell the boys I'll bring Wiggles by for a visit as soon as I've rested."

"They'll like that. Just make sure everybody stays together if you take them outside without me."

Subdued, Megan nodded. "I know you trusted me to look after Zac as well as the younger boys. I never should have divided my attention."

"Don't blame yourself. I'm the one who's ultimately responsible for everything that goes on at Camp Refuge. I should have known better."

"You mean because you let three boys visit me at once?"

"No," James said.

"Then what? Tell me?"

"Sure you want me to spell it out for you?"

"Of course."

He nodded. "Okay. My first mistake was bowing to the board and agreeing to let you come here. My second was letting you stay when I saw you'd brought your adolescent sister. I knew she'd be trouble the minute I set eyes on her. I should have sent you two packing then and there."

Megan couldn't help rising to Roxy's defense. Though she tried to tone down her rebuttal, it still came out sounding stronger than she'd wanted. "That's pure prejudice talking and you know it. Roxy's a lonely, sad little girl in a growing body. She's confused about life. Lots of teenagers go through that kind of struggle—and they don't come from homes where they're told nobody wants them around anymore."

"I did."

"I know. That's why I can't understand your attitude. All the poor kid wants is to be loved. She didn't get affection at home so she's looking elsewhere. I was hoping that working with me would show her she has value as a person. How was I to know there would be nothing but boys living here? There were girls listed on the roster when I researched this place and applied for my grant."

His eyes widened, then narrowed with the furrowing of his brow. "So, you'd intended to slip Roxy into your project all along."

"No! Nothing of the kind. I told you exactly why I included her at the last minute." Waiting for a sign he'd accepted her denial, she watched his face, hoping he'd at least give her the benefit of the doubt.

"Look, this conversation is getting us nowhere,"

James finally said. "We're both tired and edgy. If we keep it up we're liable to say things we're sorry for." He started to back away. "Get some rest. I'll see you later."

Liable to say things we're sorry for? Megan swallowed the accusation perched on the tip of her tongue. As far as she was concerned, too much had already been said, especially by James Harris.

She'd actually started to believe he'd accepted her, even liked her enough to steal a brief kiss. Well, the joke was on her. Nothing had changed. He still distrusted her theories as well as questioned her methods. And now he'd dragged her sister into the argument, blaming Roxy for being emotionally unsettled. Of course she was. The poor kid had been going through terrible trials at home.

Okay, Megan concluded, the man was entitled to his opinion, even if he was dead wrong. She couldn't do anything about his ideology. But that didn't mean she'd trust him to be unprejudiced in the future.

What she would do was continue to work with him in order to complete her project. And if she had no other choice, she'd join him again to search for the missing youngsters. But that was all. He'd made his position crystal clear. No way would she be fool enough to lower her guard and confide in him ever again. No sirree. His unfair criticism had hurt far too much.

Watching James make his way down the hill, she noticed a momentous sense of loss warring with her animosity...and winning. It didn't take much soul-searching to reveal the reason. Like it or not, Megan not only cared what he thought of her work, she wanted him to like her. To look up to her with mutual respect. To value her companionship the way she valued his. To yearn to be near her the way...

She bit her lower lip and clenched her fists to keep from giving in to the urge to call to him. There was no denying the truth she'd just found hidden in her heart. Somehow, in the midst of all the negative things that had occurred, she'd let herself fall in love.

Megan made a wry face and turned away so she couldn't see James anymore. "What a mess," she muttered in disgust. "I could have picked a dozen other camps instead of this one, and I had to come *here.*"

She spread her hands, palms up, and tilted her face to heaven. "Why did You let me do it? Huh? You know I don't want to ever get married."

The irony of her statement struck her so funny

she almost laughed. "Right. The chances of James Harris ever deciding he likes me, let alone loves me and wants to marry me, are less than zero. So there's no real problem, is there?"

Somehow, coming to that sensible conclusion didn't make her feel one smidgen better.

Chapter Eleven

By noon, Megan had managed to nap a bit then catch up on most of her chores, leaving the grooming of the animals as a treat for the children.

She'd been rehearsing what she was going to say to James when he showed up to help. Unfortunately, she didn't get to use her "Thanks, but no thanks. I can handle this by myself" speech, because he didn't return.

Calling Wiggles to keep her company, she headed for the main building to see what had delayed her promised temporary assistant. She couldn't very well banish him if he never showed up, now could she?

Struck by the absurdity of her self-defeating attitude she chuckled softly. The panting dog at her side looked up and wagged his rear half.

"You understand me, don't you, Wiggles? Sure you do. Love is real simple as far as you're concerned. As long as I feed you, pet you and scratch your back, you're happy as a kid in a candy store. I wish men were that easy to please."

The Australian shepherd nudged her hand with his nose.

Megan paused to ruffle his ears and talk to him. "I don't even want to *like* James Harris, so what am I doing dreaming of a future with him, huh? Answer me that."

Wiggles licked her hand.

"Yeah, I know. You have all the answers. Well, old buddy, I hate to tell you this but you can't solve every problem by pouring on the affection. Humans aren't that easy to influence. Besides me, I mean."

Grinning at her canine companion she gave his head one last pat and straightened. "I know what you're thinking. I'm not about to start licking James's hand in order to make him like me, so you can just forget it."

She giggled. "Boy, am I glad you can't talk like that dog in the TV commercial. I'd hate to have you telling my secrets. Then again, as smart as you are, maybe you could come up with a solution to this predicament. What do you think?"

"I think you're crazy," a deep male voice said.

For a split second, Megan's imagination attributed the comment to her dog. Then, she spotted James approaching and began to blush. *Oh, boy.* How much of her idiotic jabbering had he overheard? And what had she said that would need refuting? She wished she knew.

Joining her, he merely smiled and said, "Hi. I was just on my way to your cabin to see what was keeping you. The kids are waiting. You said you'd bring Wiggles to visit us, remember?"

Had she? Was her mind in such a chaotic state she'd forgotten a simple promise like that? Vague recollections stirred.

"I guess I did," Megan admitted. "I was so bushed, I don't remember half the stuff we talked about this morning."

"Hey, that's good."

The boyish look on his face prompted her to recall his tales of boarding school. "Don't get your hopes up, mister. I remember everything you said about horses."

"I was afraid of that."

I also remember your opinion of my sister, she thought. Having had time to calmly consider his comments, however, she'd mellowed. A lot of what he'd said made sense. Introducing Roxy into an already-unstable population of young people had been a stupid thing to do. Pure motives were not enough to mitigate a poor decision. Too bad she couldn't go back and change it.

Seated at Megan's side, the dog leaned against her leg, quietly begging for attention. She smiled down at him. "I know Wiggles will be glad to see the boys again. He's lonesome. His raccoon friends haven't been back. At least not yet."

"Good. They're usually nocturnal. If you see one out in the daylight, give it a wide berth. A change of habits can mean an animal is sick. Same goes for skunks."

"Thanks. I'll remember that." She gave the dog a hand signal releasing it to run ahead as she started down the hill.

James fell into step beside her. "You look much better. Did you get some sleep?"

"A little. How about you?"

"Enough. Aaron woke me to tell me the sheriff's team was about to pull out. They just left."

Megan took a deep breath and released it as a noisy sigh. "Can't say that's a surprise after I told them about losing my jacket. Maybe I shouldn't have said anything. What if I was mistaken?"

"Were you?"

She pulled a face. "No. It's gone, and nobody

would have taken it but Roxy. So, what do we do now?"

"Rely on volunteers. Some of the ones who were here all along need to get back to their jobs but others will come. Inez is going to speak to the brotherhood group at her church and get them involved. We'll have plenty more help before nightfall."

"How will we feed them all?"

"No problem. Word's gotten out that we're hosting rescuers. You should see the stacks of donated food in the kitchen. Inez won't have to cook a thing for weeks."

"My college church group used to do good deeds like that. We joked that we ought to hand out covered casserole dishes to new members because they were going to need them if they planned to fit in."

"Sounds like Inez and her friends. They're always baking something for somebody in need. Most of the extra food probably did come from church groups. It figures. Folks around here are pretty religious."

Megan grinned. "Yeah, well… Just because a person acts pious or calls himself a Christian, doesn't mean he is, as you well know. Lots of folks warm a pew on Sundays without a spiritual connection to Jesus Christ. It doesn't make them bad people. It's just sad that they're missing so much of the joy they could have if they were really a part of Him."

"I suppose you're alluding to my parents."

"Hey, if the pew fits…" Megan giggled.

"Okay, okay." He led the way onto the porch of the dining hall and held the door for her.

Pausing, Megan glanced at her dog. "Can Wiggles come in, too?"

"Not if he's still shedding," James said. "Why don't I bring the boys out here and let them brush him?"

"Good idea. I'll go get my grooming tools."

"No need. We'll find something you can use. Wait here. I'll be right back."

"Okay. Fine." She plunked down on the top porch step, her feet on the next one down. Wiggles joined her and laid his chin on her lap while she absently stroked his thick fur. Every pass of her hand swept off more loose hair, piling it up in a nest of mottled gray fuzz at the base of his spine.

"You? Shedding? Naw," she said, shaking her fingers and watching the accumulation drift away on the breeze. James might not realize it but keeping the dog outside wasn't going to help much. The more the boys brushed him, the more dog hair was going to stick to them—and to anything they touched—not to mention becoming airborne and drifting into who knows where. Living with an animal the size of an Australian shepherd during shedding season and trying to keep a clean house, was like trying to pile up loose feathers with a snowblower!

The screen door banged. Mark and Kyle were the first ones out. Each jockeyed for available space next to Wiggles, shoving and shouting until the dog sought safety on the opposite side of Megan.

"Whoa. One at a time," she ordered, standing. "You're going to have to be more polite if you want to pet Wiggles. You're scaring him."

"Me first," Mark hollered.

"No! Me, me," Kyle countered.

"Neither one of you deserves to be first when you act like that," Megan said. "Now simmer down, okay? Mr. Harris has gone to find a brush we can use. Until he gets back, you can both pet the dog if you do it quietly and gently."

The boys muttered a reply in unison. Megan chose to interpret their mumbling as "Yes, ma'am."

"All right. And as soon as Bobby Joe and the others get here, they get a turn. Understand?"

"Yes, ma'am."

Although she was keeping a close eye on the boys, she nevertheless sensed James's return. Aaron, Bobby Joe, Robbie and John were with him. The two littlest campers looked happy but Bobby Joe wore an expression of impending doom that made her heart hurt.

Forcing a smile of greeting, she addressed James. "Did you find a brush we can use?"

"Not yet. Why don't you stay here with Aaron and the guys? I'll run up to your place and get your dog-grooming stuff. Just tell me where to look."

"Okay. You'll find two red-handled brushes in a footlocker next to the horse pen." Her grin brightened. "Think you can stand getting that close?"

"I'll manage."

Megan was watching James's determined pace, and laughing to herself, when she noticed that Bobby Joe had stepped forward and begun to slowly brush Wiggles. It occurred to her that he might be using his own hairbrush, but so what? It was far more important to let him express himself by caring for the dog than it was to correct him for using the wrong tool.

Soap and water would fix the brush.

Only unconditional love and acceptance could mend the child.

* * *

The roar James let out when he returned with the dog's slicker brush and saw what had happened in his absence would have been frightening…if it hadn't been so funny. Megan no longer had to wonder whose personal hairbrush had been pressed into service. Everyone knew.

"I'll wash it for you later," she said, giggling. "I didn't know. Honest."

"Never mind. I'd rather use my comb than have to pick ticks out of my hair."

"That's probably wise. Did you say hello to Buckets while you were up the hill?"

James's scowl deepened. "Don't push it, lady."

"Sorry. I know it's not polite to laugh but I couldn't help myself. You should have seen the look on your face when you got back."

"At least you had the courtesy to act surprised."

"I was. Believe me. Bobby Joe brought that brush outside with him. By the time I realized he wasn't just petting the dog, it was already too late."

"We agree there." He glared at Aaron. "I suppose you don't know a thing about this."

The young man shrugged. "Nope."

"Didn't think so. Okay. Everybody can take a turn brushing the dog as long as you're done by six. When you wash up for supper, make sure you get all the loose hair off you."

Even later, after she'd joined the group for their evening meal, Megan had to fight to keep from bursting into giggles. Nearly every time she glanced at James he was frowning and picking or brushing some unseen object off one of the kids or himself.

She didn't need a microscope to tell her he thought he saw dog hair and probably one or two seed ticks, too. Chances were very good he wasn't imagining a thing.

Several truckloads of volunteer rescuers arrived and trooped into the dining hall just as Inez was serving dessert.

The men were mostly well seasoned, Megan noted, with a few gangly teens bringing up the rear, apparently in deference to their elders. Everyone wore camouflage clothing of one type or another, hiking boots and a bright orange base-ball cap, which they failed to remove, even indoors. The "uniform" was a familiar sight, especially during official Arkansas hunting seasons.

Megan listened carefully, determined to remember who was who, as James introduced each man in turn. It soon became clear how impossible that goal was. Not only did some of them share the same last name, Inez kept butting in to explain their extended family connections, leaving Megan totally confused.

In self-defense, she finally resorted to simply smiling and offering a heartfelt "Thank you for coming."

James paused and beamed as a late arrival entered. Instead of shaking hands, the men greeted each other with backslapping and a brief hug, much to Megan's surprise.

"This is my old friend Graydon Payne," James told her. "His wife, Stacy, trains search-and-rescue dogs."

"Oh, how wonderful!" Megan was filled with relief and thankfulness. "Is she outside?"

The tall man took her hand, held it and slowly shook his head. "No. She's on assignment in South America. There was a bad earthquake down there. Stacy took a team of dogs and handlers to help locate buried victims." He gave James a sober look. "She'd be here if she could."

"I know," James answered. "That's why I called you. The sheriff swore there weren't any tracking dogs available. I figured contacting you in person was worth a try."

He looked to Megan. "I didn't tell you what I was doing because I didn't want to get your hopes up for nothing."

Sniffling, she stood tall and managed a smile. "Trying to help is never for nothing, even if it doesn't work out." A tear escaped and rolled down her cheek. She dashed it away. "Thank you for calling your friend. It means a lot to me."

She turned to face Graydon and the others. "And thank you again for coming. All of you. I know you have jobs and families of your own to think about. I'll be ready to go in a few minutes. I just need to change."

"Not tonight," Graydon said. "I may not use my nose to sniff out missing people the way my wife's dogs do but I've been on enough searches to have learned some important lessons. Tired rescuers make mistakes. Miss things they'd see if they were rested. Sometimes they even become part of the problem by getting lost or hurt."

"I had a nap today," Megan said.

James gently took her hand. "That's not enough. Gray and I talked this over when I phoned him. You and I will stay here and sleep while the rest of them spend the night searching the woods. Tomorrow, they'll come in and we'll take their place."

"I'm rested enough to go tonight," she insisted. "I have to. It's my sister out there."

"That's exactly why you should stay here," James told her. "If…*when* we find Roxy, she'll need you to be at your best, not run-down. You can't take care of her if you're in worse shape than she is."

"But…"

Graydon nodded sagely and stood his ground. "James is right. He went through the same kind of thing with me a few years ago. I had to learn the hard way. Almost killed myself packing an injured dog back to camp on my shoulders." He gave an exaggerated shrug, then stretched. "It still hurts sometimes. Probably always will. If I'd used my head, I wouldn't have been in that situation in the first place."

Megan had run out of valid arguments. She got along with domestic animals just fine but she didn't possess much wilderness experience. If she chose to defy James and his friend and sneak out on her own, she might very well become another statistic, as they'd warned.

"All right. I'll wait here," she said. "If I can't sleep, I'll spend the night praying you find Zac and my sister."

"Now you're talking," Graydon said with a

smile. "I knew you and I were on the same team the minute I met you."

James didn't go to bed as early as usual that night. He had too much on his mind. Instead, he sank into the porch swing he and Megan had shared, gave it a push with his feet and closed his eyes so he could think without distraction.

Some of the things Megan had been saying about God were starting to make sense. He didn't like admitting that, even to himself. If he viewed his parents as clueless lost souls instead of saints with tarnished halos, who was there left to hate? Certainly not the brothers he'd tried so hard to best when they were all children.

Of course, he could always blame God for whatever had gone wrong, assuming He existed in the first place. His old buddy Graydon obviously thought so.

James pictured himself as a little boy. The only reason he'd accompanied his family to church was because his brothers were always getting praise for their participation. Still, a few random Bible verses stuck in his memory. So did the premise that there might actually be a heavenly Father who cared about him, although why God would bother with a guy like him made no sense.

As a child, he remembered weeping and praying for his parents to take his side for once. They never did. Yet, looking back, he wondered what his life would have been like if he'd remained in that family. Maybe Megan was right. Maybe they had done him a favor by kicking him out. If he'd stayed in such a destructive home the experience might well have broken his spirit.

His breath caught. Could his prayers actually have been answered? Was it possible that a loving Father had looked after the soul of a miserable little boy by *not* giving him the loving home and parental acceptance he'd begged for?

That train of thought gave James the shivers. Looking back on his life, he was starting to see a logical progression of events. But what about the future? If God was willing to help a confused kid like he'd been, why wasn't He doing something for Megan? She didn't deserve the ordeal her sister was putting her through.

James knew, if there was any way to ease her suffering, he'd act in a heartbeat. The best search teams in northern Arkansas had already tried and failed to find those kids. What could he, one man, possibly accomplish alone?

Beginning to pray wasn't a conscious decision. One moment James was merely worrying about

Megan and the next he was interceding with the Lord on her behalf.

"Well, God, I guess I'll take a chance You're really out there," he said quietly.

Oh, nice one, Harris. Make Him mad right off the bat.

"I mean, thanks for taking care of me when I was a dumb kid. As You can see, I haven't gotten much smarter. But I know Megan needs help and I don't know who else to ask."

That's better. Not good, but better. Don't stop now.

"I've done all I know to do. Everybody has. How about it? Where'd Roxy and Zac go?"

I don't know what else to say, James thought, filled with disgust at his weak attempt to contact God. His eyes suddenly felt damp. He blinked, staring into the infinity of the starry night sky.

"I don't know what You want with the likes of me but here I am. Show me what to do and I'll do it. Anything. I mean it. Just please, please help Megan."

James waited in silence, his breathing shallow, his pulse remarkably even, considering his heightened senses.

Every nerve in his body told him something momentous had occurred, yet he hadn't seen or heard anything unusual. No heavenly trumpets had sounded. No moving finger wrote answers or warnings on the walls the way it had in Old Testament days. As a matter of fact, the longer he sat there, the more tranquil he felt.

Suddenly weary beyond belief, he got to his feet, walked slowly into the dorm and went to bed, hoping for the relief of sleep.

Chapter Twelve

Megan had lain down on top of her coverlet, intending to rest a few minutes before showering and getting ready for bed. The next thing she knew, night had fallen and thunder was rumbling in distance.

For an instant after she opened her eyes she didn't know where she was. Then lightning flashed, revealing details of the small cabin.

Her first conscious thought was *Roxy's out in this awful weather. Good thing she took my jacket.*

Rapid pounding at her door brought her fully awake. Wiggles bristled and growled.

"Who is it?"

"Me. James. Open up."

Megan's heart was in her throat. She jerked open the door. "Roxy! Have they found her?"

"No."

Any comfort she might have drawn from the man's presence was counteracted by the unsettling sight that greeted her. James's dark hair was tousled, his clothing was rumpled and he bore a wild-eyed expression that seemed to intensify every time lightning flashed.

"What's the matter, then?" Megan stepped back to admit him. "You'd better come in. Looks like a bad storm."

"I know. That makes it worse—I think." Pacing across the cabin he quickly ran out of room and turned to retrace his steps.

"Makes what worse?"

"Everything. Nothing. I don't know."

Megan grabbed his arm and stopped him as he passed. "If you don't stand still and tell me what's going on I'm going to have a hissy fit right here and now."

"Okay, okay. It was a dream…I think. Only, I've never had one like it before. You know how things in dreams are all blurred and vague and confusing? This wasn't like that. Everything was crystal clear. I was drifting off to sleep when I suddenly remembered."

"Remembered what?"

"A place I came across a long time ago, down by the river. I hadn't thought of it in years."

"You woke me up and scared me silly to tell me that? Why? Did you dream Roxy and Zac were there?"

"No. I told you it was weird."

"You're what's weird," Megan said flatly.

"I know. And I'm not real crazy about the feeling. All I know is, I need to go there."

She frowned and peered out the window. The first wind-driven, quarter-size drops of rain were smacking the panes, merging and starting to dribble down. "Now? In this weather? You must be out of your mind."

"Probably," James answered. "But I'm going anyway. I'll need four-wheel drive, so that means taking the ATV. The country I'm headed for is way too rough for a truck. Hiking in would take way too long."

"What about the searchers? You're the one who told me we should stay in camp and let them do their job. Won't they be checking the area you're worried about?"

"No. It's too far away. Too out of the ordinary. I haven't been there in years, myself. I don't know what brought the place to mind tonight."

"The memory was probably hovering there in your subconscious all the time, waiting for you to acknowledge it," she said. "If you were drifting off to sleep, your customary defenses were shutting down. That's how the idea leaked out."

"You're telling me my brain leaks?"

Megan gave him a patient smile. "In a manner of speaking. The human mind can make imaginary things seem very real, especially when we're under a lot of stress. I'm not saying you shouldn't follow up on your idea. I just mean you don't need to rush."

James paused to rake his fingers through his hair.

"There's something else. Something I haven't told you."

She could tell he was struggling with whatever he was trying to say so she reassured him. "Go ahead. I'm a trained listener, remember?"

"I don't even know where to start. Or where to end."

"Well, how about the stuff in between?" Megan asked. She schooled her features to reflect calm acceptance. "Take a deep breath and just start talking. We can sort out the details and make sense of everything later."

James arched his eyebrows and almost smiled. "Oh, yeah? I seriously doubt that. You see, it all started when I decided to take a chance and talk to God."

* * *

Flabbergasted, Megan listened to James's confusing tale. He didn't employ commonly used religious terminology or realize what a big step he'd taken, but his story was a familiar one. When he'd consciously offered himself to the Lord and volunteered to be of service, no matter what, he'd begun a new life. That shed a totally different light on his apparent revelation.

"I don't get the connection, assuming there even is one," he concluded, "but I'm positive I'm supposed to go check those caves."

"Caves?" Megan's pulse jumped into high gear. "I thought you said the place you remembered was down by the river."

"It is. That's part of the problem. I remember noticing marks on the inside walls from previous floods. If this storm develops the way I think it will, it'll dump so much runoff into the Spring River, those cave openings will end up under water. No telling how long they'll stay blocked like that."

"Why didn't you say so? Let me grab my shoes. I'll go with you."

"No. You stay here. It's too dangerous."

Megan rolled her eyes at him. "Dangerous? Ha! You don't know me very well, do you?"

"It's you who don't know me," James countered. "The only reason I came to tell you where I was going was so you could explain to Aaron in the morning—in case I'm not back by then."

"You couldn't leave him a note?"

"Don't argue."

"Me? You're the one who's being unreasonable. Roxy rode double with Aaron on that stupid ATV of yours. There's no good reason why I can't do the same with you."

"The best reason I can think of is that I told you to stay here," James said flatly. "I'm not going on a joyride. There's no trail, it's pitch-dark outside and it's going to be a miserable, wet trip. I'll make much better time if I don't have to worry about taking care of you."

"Nobody asked you to take care of me. I'll be responsible for myself."

"Like you were responsible for your sister?"

Megan bit her lip. "That was a low blow."

"Yes, it was. I'm sorry it was necessary. But I had to break through that stubbornness of yours and make you listen. If Roxy and Zac happen to be hiding in the caves, which I actually doubt, the sooner I warn them about the danger of rising water, the better. If they're not there, I'll turn right around and head for home. Either way, you'd slow me down too much."

He strode to the door and flung it open. "It's that simple."

"There's nothing simple about any of this," Megan shouted after him.

The force of the gusting wind nearly tore the door from her grasp. She slammed it by throwing her whole body into the effort.

Tears stung her eyes. It wasn't fair. Roxy was family. Her only sister. She'd promised their mother she'd take care of the girl and she'd failed. There was only one way to make amends, and that was to suffer whatever indignities and uncertainties were necessary in order to put things right.

Filled with a burst of courage and enthusiasm, Megan slid her bare feet into her sneakers and tied the laces rapidly. Wiggles immediately headed for the door, anticipating an outing.

"Sorry, boy. You need to stay here," she said. "I'm going to leave two notes for Aaron, one on the table and one tied to your collar. That way, when somebody comes looking for me, they're sure to spot one of them."

Hurrying, she finished the brief notes then tore open a package containing a disposable poncho and slid the thin plastic garment over her head. It wasn't as durable as a regular raincoat would have been but it was perfect for what she had in mind. If James wouldn't take her to the river and let her see for herself that Roxy wasn't in trouble, she'd make like a pioneer and get there the old-fashioned way.

As expected, Buckets was standing in the rain by choice, letting the pelting drops scratch her back and looking thoroughly contented.

Megan managed to bridle the horse before she heard the distinctive rev of the ATV. To be leaving that quickly, the hardheaded camp director must have run all the way home.

"Oh, please, not yet. I need a few more minutes."

The engine noise built, then grew fainter. Megan knew, if she didn't mount up immediately, she'd lose her chance to follow successfully.

Gathering the reins in her left hand, she stepped onto the top of the footlocker, swung her right leg over the horse's slippery bare back and pulled herself astride.

If James had given her more time she'd gladly have saddled up before risking a long ride in the rain. Unfortunately, she no longer had that choice. Or any other.

She gave Buckets a nudge with her heels and

leaned forward to offer encouragement. "Okay, girl. Come on. Let's go. You and I have a job to do."

If Megan hadn't been so worried about being left behind, she'd have chuckled at the next remark that popped into her head. It was straight out of the movies.

She gripped hard with her knees, hung on to the horse's mane and said, "Follow that car!"

Megan had assumed she'd have little trouble trailing something as noisy as the ATV. At first, that was true. The farther they got from the camp, however, the harder it was to pinpoint the direction James was headed. Sound echoed erratically, bouncing off the hillsides and sliding down the valleys.

Thunder did more than rumble in the distance. It shook the ground. A crack of lightning split the night air, setting Megan's hair on end and making her shiver in spite of the humidity trapped beneath her plastic poncho.

"Oh, please, Lord. Take care of us," she prayed aloud. "All of us. I know I shouldn't have brought Buckets out in this storm but I can't quit now. I don't know where I am."

The absolute truth of that confession sent a shudder of fear zinging through her from head to toe. In the daylight, given enough time, she might have been able to eventually find her way back to Camp Refuge, especially if she'd paid attention to landmarks she'd passed on the way. At night, in the midst of a storm, it was impossible to have seen anything distinctive, let alone taken special note of it.

Going back was not an option. Then again, she wasn't looking forward to being stuck out there all by herself, either. It was imperative she catch up to James, or at least get close enough to keep him in sight until he'd reached his goal.

Megan's main advantage was her mode of transportation. Buckets was cautious and sure-footed, which allowed them to cut across rough terrain that was impassable by motorized vehicle. More than once she wondered if she'd worked too far into a thicket of saplings and vines to continue, but each time she came out the other side closer to the sound of the ATV.

By listening carefully she could tell every time James was scaling a hill or traversing an especially rocky area. Once he was through it, the revving of the engine always evened out.

Suddenly, the noise from the ATV stopped. She nudged Buckets harder, urged her up the last few feet of the slope they'd been climbing and halted at the crest.

Lightning shot across the sky in a jagged show of force. Thunder rumbled from all sides. Rain pelted down in waves, as if hurled from the clouds by an angry giant.

Nevertheless, Megan sat tall and peered into the distance. Across the next narrow ravine a pair of stationary lights gleamed. Could that be the ATV?

"Probably. Unless white-tail deer come equipped with headlights these days," she answered aloud. "Come on, Buckets. Let's go tell Mr. Harris he's got company."

By the time Megan reached the vehicle it was abandoned. Twenty or thirty yards ahead she could see the beam of a flashlight and catch an occasional glimpse of a yellow slicker moving among the trees.

She cupped her hands around her mouth and shouted, "James! Wait. Where are you going?"

The light stopped moving.

"James. It's me," she called again, relieved when she saw the light swing around to point at her. Hooray! He was coming back!

"What are you doing out here?" he yelled.

"Following you," Megan answered as soon as

he drew nearer. "Good thing I caught you before you started off on foot or I'd have lost your trail. Is this the place you told me about?"

"No."

"Then why did you stop?"

He pointed the light at the rear of the ATV. "Flat tire. I must've hit a sharp rock."

"Out here? Rocks? No kidding. This place is nothing *but* rocks."

"You didn't answer my question. What are you doing here?"

"Yes, I did. I said I followed you. You wouldn't take me with you so I got here on my own. Well, almost on my own. Buckets helped a little."

"I can see that."

"She is a little hard to overlook."

Megan instinctively ducked and hugged her horse's neck as another bright bolt zigzagged across the sky.

"You're an idiot," James yelled over the ensuing thunder. "You shouldn't be out in this weather."

"Takes one to know one. How much farther?"

"I'm not sure. Maybe three or four miles. I'll recognize the place when I see it."

"Okay. Hop on."

"Do *what?*"

"Mount up behind me. You'll be fine. It won't hurt Buckets to carry us both for a little while."

"Fine? In your dreams, lady. I don't ride horses, remember?"

"Hey, I'm not the one who insisted there was such a big rush—you were. Is there or isn't there a chance somebody could drown if we're late getting there?"

"A remote one."

"Are you willing to take that risk?" Megan asked knowingly. She could feel the tension, sense the emotional struggle he was having. To his credit, the hand holding the flashlight remained steady.

James raised the beam briefly to her face, then lowered it and traced the outline of the placid beast beneath her. "There's no saddle!"

"You left camp so fast I didn't have time for one," Megan said. "It'll be fine. All we need is a stump or a big rock for you to stand on. I'll bring Buckets in close and you can just step aboard. It's easy."

"Oh? And what keeps me there? She's as fat and round as a barrel. Even without all this rain her back would be slippery."

"You—you can hang on to me."

Megan swallowed hard, hoping James hadn't

noticed the unexpected quaver in her voice. He might not have had any experience riding double, but she knew what to expect. The motion of the horse was going to slide them into close proximity. *Very* close proximity.

Suddenly, she wasn't certain she should allow the camp director to join her, especially since he was so upset. Then again, his anger would provide a good buffer. Anything was better than having him relax and enjoy himself while she fought to remain aloof.

That logical reasoning helped settle her nerves. "Okay, suit yourself. Walk if you want to," she said flatly. "Just stop wasting time. The sooner we get to the caves, the sooner we stop being targets for all this lightning. Am I right?"

"Unfortunately."

Mumbling to himself, James cast around for a platform, spotted a nearby stump and climbed up on it.

Allowing him no opportunity to change his mind, Megan maneuvered the horse into position. "Okay, we're ready. Grab her mane with your left hand and hang on tight, then swing your right leg around and aim to land behind me, like the cowboys do in the movies. Centrifugal force will take care of the rest."

"Yeah, right."

"Just do it."

"Okay, okay."

James took a deep breath, tensed every muscle and flung himself at the horse's side. He hit with an "Oof" and a muttered expletive.

Startled, Buckets shifted her balance and side-stepped. Megan tightened the reins. "Whoa! Easy, baby. Easy."

"Hold her still," James yelled.

"I'm trying. I didn't know you were going to tackle her like a football player."

"I just did what you told me to."

"Not very well."

"I haven't had much practice, okay?"

She glanced over her shoulder to see why his voice sounded as if it were coming from somewhere below. It was. The poor guy had a doubtful hold at best. His effort to mount had brought his right ankle barely past midpoint on the horse's spine and his other foot was kicking empty air. Even if she could maneuver him back onto the stump, Megan doubted he'd make a second attempt.

"Here," she said, grasping his left forearm near the elbow and lifting with all her might.

By leaning back, she was able to give him

enough leverage to finish mounting. When he slid into place, however, she was left hanging off the opposite side.

James righted her effortlessly. "Watch yourself."

"I'm fine. You just take care of your half of the horse."

"I'd rather push a truck."

Megan was at the end of her patience. She was cold, wet, tempted beyond reason by a situation not of her own making, and too exhausted by the whole ordeal to put up with his complaining.

"Knock it off, mister. You could be up to your boot tops in mud and ducking to keep from getting toasted by lightning, instead of riding to the caves on this wonderful horse."

"We're not there yet," James countered. "If you weren't out here, too, I'd gladly take my chances on foot."

"If I wasn't here you'd have no *choice* but to walk."

He rocked from side to side on the slick hide, inching himself away from her. "I meant, I wouldn't be concerned about getting a little fried."

"My, my. You do like to live dangerously, don't you?"

"I must," he said wryly. "I got on a horse with you, didn't I?"

Chapter Thirteen

Megan was so bumfuzzled by riding close to James she didn't know whether she wanted to laugh, cry or scream. Or all of the above.

The man perched behind her was evidently doing his best to keep from touching her, which might mean he wanted to avoid her as much as possible. Or, it could mean he cared about her, respected her high principles and didn't want to do anything that would give her the wrong impression of his own standards.

Then again, maybe he was holding back because he was as unsure of her feelings as she was of his. All she'd have to do to find out was lean back a tiny bit and rest her shoulders against his chest. Just for a second. That would be long enough. And maybe lay her head on his shoulder?

The idea was so tempting it made her shiver. It was also risky. If James rejected her, she knew it would hurt terribly—not to mention embarrass them both.

What am I doing even thinking about my personal life at a time like this? Megan asked herself. *What kind of monster am I? My sister's missing. Roxy should be the only one on my mind.*

But Roxy wasn't the only one, was she? Like it or not, James Harris now occupied a major portion of Megan's thoughts—and of her dreams. Falling for him wasn't a choice she'd made by sensible reasoning. It had simply happened, slowly, unconsciously, yet more quickly than she'd ever imagined it could.

Love wasn't nearly this complicated in her favorite novels, Megan reflected, frustrated by her indecisiveness. She was a bold, independent, educated woman, with her feet on the ground and career choices ahead. She didn't need any man to make her complete. So what was she afraid of?

Moreover, what was James afraid of? If she didn't gather her courage and force the issue soon she might never find out, and that would be turning her back on a God-given opportunity.

She sent out a silent *Lord, help me* and cleared her throat, preparing to tell James exactly how she felt about him. When she opened her mouth to speak, however, what popped out was "How much farther to the caves?"

"Maybe half a mile." He pointed with the flashlight. "Take that path over there. It should lead down to the river."

Down? her mind echoed. *Down, as in steep?* Had her unspoken plea been answered already? She certainly hoped so, because she obviously couldn't count on herself for anything. What had become of the capable, levelheaded person she'd been just days ago? She wished she knew!

Bringing Buckets to the crest of the ridge, Megan halted. "Looks safe enough except for a few low branches. Keep your head down and hang on. This could get a little rough."

Not wanting to give James time to come up with an alternative plan and spoil her chance to force him to embrace her, she nudged the horse with her heels and they started over the lip of the hill.

Head down, Buckets picked her way cautiously, stiffly, around protruding rocks. The motion was anything but smooth. Still, James refused to lay a hand on Megan. The more their momentum propelled them forward, the farther back he leaned.

"Sorry," he said. "It's hard to stay… Uh-oh."

Megan felt him start to slide sideways. "If you were hanging on like I told you to, you wouldn't be having problems."

"I didn't think—"

Just then, Buckets's foot slipped. The mare jerked to right herself, throwing both riders off balance.

Megan would have been able to cope with the abrupt movement if James hadn't chosen that moment to finally make a grab for her. She screeched, "Let go!" on her way down.

The next few seconds passed in a blur. James hit the ground first. Megan landed partially on top of him.

Buckets skidded to a halt and looked back at them as if to say, "What're you doing way down there?"

"Are you okay?" James asked, breathless.

"I guess so." Scooting aside and sitting up, Megan rubbed her hands on her jeans to clean them off before wiping her wet face with the backs of her wrists. "You picked a fine time to take my advice."

"Hey, I'm not the one who left camp without a saddle. At least you had her mane. There was nothing for me to hang on to *except* you."

"Exactly. And you did your level best to keep from touching me, didn't you?"

"Yes, I did." James stood and held out his hand.

Megan clambered to her feet without accepting his help, thankful the drizzle and the darkness masked her unsteady emotions. "At least you admit it."

"I plan to admit a lot of things once we're back in camp," he said solemnly. "Right now, I can see it's a good thing we fell off when we did. I almost missed that old corner post over there."

He shined the flashlight for her. "See? Down by the big cedar? If there's a surveyor's mark on it we've found the right place."

"I—I think I see a post." She sniffled and took a disgusted swipe at the salty drops mixed with the rain trickling down her cheeks.

"That's the landmark I was looking for. The cave entrances are a few yards south. We can walk from here."

"Anything to keep from getting back on a horse?"

James snorted. "No. Anything to keep from going crazy trying to behave myself when I'm that close to you."

Her eyes widened. Did that mean what she hoped it did?

"You weren't trying to stay away from me because you didn't like me?"

"Ha! I should be so lucky." He grabbed her hand and started off. "Come on. We've wasted enough time."

The logical side of Megan's mind kept insisting they were on a wild-goose chase, no matter what James had dreamed or imagined. The side that believed in divine intervention wasn't nearly as convinced, especially since they'd taken their tumble in such a fortuitous place.

She struggled to keep pace with his longer strides while Buckets trailed them both, head hung low, like a faithful dog following its master.

"Don't you feel a little silly racing around the woods like this?" Megan asked. "I mean, nobody's given us a good reason to think we'd find anything here, have they?"

"I told you I couldn't explain the urge to investigate. Call it intuition if you want."

"Suppose you're wrong."

"Then I'll feel silly and you'll get to gloat," James said. "I'm willing to take that chance."

"Good for you." She held tighter to his hand. "I like a man with the courage of his convictions."

"Do you? Well, well. I thought you hated my stubborn streak. Didn't you call me opinionated?"

"Yes. Just because I admire your character

doesn't mean I think you're always right. You can be self-confident and still be dead wrong, you know."

"Are you speaking from experience, Ms. White?"

"Not me. I'm never wrong, remember?"

James started to chuckle, then abruptly stopped. "Listen. Hear that?"

She strained. "No. What?"

"Voices. Over that way, I think."

"I don't hear a thing."

"That's because you're always talking. Hush."

"Yes, sir," she mumbled, half-disgusted. He must have the ears of an owl if he could hear anything over all the background noise. The heart of the storm had moved on, taking most of the thunder and lightning with it, but rain was still beating down on the trees and the rush of the river had become a roar.

Megan jumped when James suddenly cupped his hands around his mouth and shouted, "Zac! Zac, it's me."

She looked up at his profile silhouetted against the gray sky. *For his sake, let him get some kind of response, even if it isn't the one he expects.*

Struck by the negative tone of her appeal, she wondered if maybe she hadn't been viewing this situation through the murky veil of her own pride. Right now, it seemed James's faith was a lot stronger than hers. Even if he was mistaken, the least she could do was give his efforts her full support.

"Roxy!" Megan called.

Beside her, James momentarily froze, then took off running. "This way!"

Though she still hadn't heard anything to get excited about, she followed. The beam of his flashlight bounced over the uneven ground and danced among the trees up ahead like a sunbeam riding a bucking bronco. And speaking of horses, Megan wished she was aboard Buckets instead of picking her own way on foot across a forest floor littered with rocks and recently downed branches. No telling what dangers lay hidden beneath the carpet of wet leaves—not to mention the usual complement of ticks and chiggers.

Caution slowed her enough that James reached the riverbank before she did. He threw himself to the ground, facedown, head and shoulders hanging over the edge.

Megan was worried he'd fallen until she heard him shout, "Roxanne!"

Her breath caught. Her heart raced. The certainty in his voice said it all. They'd found her sister!

Woozy with relief, Megan was afraid she was about to keel over. Before her emotions could overpower her will, she dropped to her knees next to James, hoping to see what he was seeing. It was no use. She was too short. She thumped his back to get his attention. "Is it really Roxy?"

"Yes." James raised on one elbow. "Zac, too. They look okay so far but they won't be for long. I'm an idiot. I left my rope on the ATV."

Rope? Rope? Think! "How long a piece do you need?"

"The longer the better. Why?"

"Buckets's reins might work. Wait. I'll get them."

She returned with the whole bridle. "Let me unfasten the reins from the bit. It'll just take a minute."

"No time. We'll use it like that," James said. "Stretch it out and tie one end to that little hickory tree. It may bend some under my weight but it won't break. It takes a tornado to snap a hickory that size."

"What're you going to do?" Her eyes widened when she realized he'd already removed his boots. She stared past him at the river. Broken patches of white froth were clear indications of how fast the water was now traveling. "You're not going in there!"

"Unless you have a better idea. Those kids don't dare try to climb out by themselves." He whipped off the slicker and threw it aside. "They'd be swept away the minute they set foot in the water."

Even knowing he'd made the right decision, Megan had to fight the urge to beg him to reconsider. She nodded. "Okay. How can I help? Tell me exactly what to do."

"Make sure your end of the rein doesn't come loose. I'll have to climb partway, then swing in. I don't want to end up floating downriver instead."

"Got it. What else?" There was a telltale tremor in her voice.

"They've got a little fire going in the cave so I'll be able to see. You keep the flashlight. I'll bring Roxy out first. Be ready to help her climb after I boost her up."

He hesitated, laid a hand tenderly on Megan's arm. "Just don't fall in, okay? I don't want to lose you."

She managed a slight smile. "Be careful."

"I will. We have a date to discuss some important things and I don't plan to miss it."

Before Megan could reply he gave her a quick kiss on the cheek, levered himself over the bank and disappeared from view.

* * *

Teeth gritted, muscles straining, James eased closer to the water and prepared to leap toward the cave opening. He must do this perfectly. Failure was unthinkable. Everybody was counting on him. Especially Megan.

Was this what it was like to trust God? He sure hoped so because he was about to do something totally crazy.

With a muttered "Here goes," he jumped.

The makeshift rope stretched but held. His wet hands started to slip, then gripped.

Roxy was crouched in the cave opening, waiting. She snatched at his ankle to stop him from going backward.

James dropped to the ground beside her. The sobbing girl clutched his hand. "Oh, Mr. Harris, am I glad to see you. I didn't know what to do. The water kept coming up. I was afraid we'd drown."

"You still might if you don't do exactly as I say."

"I will, I will. I promise." Her tears glistened in the flickering firelight.

James wanted to throw his arms around both kids and hug them senseless, but that kind of reunion would have to wait. So would recriminations. First, they had to escape the rising flood. And the sooner the better.

He spotted Zac in the rear of the cave. The boy was wrapped in Megan's missing red jacket and reclining next to the fire. "Zac. Get over here. I need your help."

"Sorry," Zac said. "I can't."

Roxy grabbed James's arm and tugged him forward. "That's what I was trying to tell you, Mr. Harris. Zac's hurt. He can't walk. See? It's all my fault."

"What do you mean he's hurt?"

"His leg. I tried to put a splint on it but I couldn't get it right. And I couldn't leave him and go for help. What if I got lost? What if I couldn't find my way back? He'd die!"

James had dropped to his knees beside the boy as Roxy chattered on. Gently, he probed the injury site to assess the damage. "It might be just a bad sprain. Did anything break the skin?"

"No," Zac said, flinching. "Ouch!"

"Okay. How do you feel otherwise?" James laid his hand on the boy's forehead. "You're feverish. When did you hurt your leg? Right after you two ran away?"

"We didn't… Oh, never mind. Yeah. That same day." Zac's teeth chattered. "Man, it's cold in here. Can we go home now?"

"That's the plan," James told him, straightening. "I'm going to hand Roxy up to her sister first, then come back for you. Think you can wait that long?"

"Like, where am I gonna go?"

James huffed. "I see you haven't lost your sarcastic sense of humor."

The teen gave him a knowing grin. "You'd wonder what was wrong with me if I didn't give you a hard time."

Touched by Zac's candor and warmed by his smile, James nodded. "You're right, you little hoodlum."

"Hey, watch it with the 'little' stuff."

"Right now," James said, sobering, "I'm glad you're not any bigger. Looks like I'm going to have to pack you out of here on my back."

"No way." The boy folded his arms across his chest. "I'll just wait for the water to go down and get me a crutch or something."

"Then I hope you can swim," James replied, pointing. "See that line halfway up the wall? That's how deep it's going to get in here."

Behind him, he heard Roxy's sharp intake of breath. "We have to get out!"

"That's what I've been trying to tell you," James said. He took her hand and led her back to the cave opening. Water was beginning to slosh in, wetting the floor in a widening circle. The river was rising even faster than he'd expected. There was no time to waste.

He grabbed the end of the leather rein and gave it a tug to make sure it was still solidly anchored, then leaned out and called, "Megan. You ready?"

When there was no answering shout, James thought his heart was going to pound its way out of his chest.

"Megan! Answer me."

Chapter Fourteen

Perched above the cave, Megan strained to listen. Several times she'd imagined hearing James's voice, had answered and had discovered she'd been mistaken.

When she heard something this time, she crawled cautiously to the edge of the bank and used the flashlight to signal. "James? I'm here."

Beside her, the makeshift rescue rope tightened, creaking against the sturdy hickory sapling she'd used as its anchor.

James's voice came to her like a breath on the wind. "I'm sending Roxy up. Get ready to grab her."

"Okay. All set."

Reaching over the bank, Megan laid the flashlight on the ground and used her other hand to steady the leather strap, hoping that if it did slip she'd be quick enough and strong enough to catch and hold it.

Icy, trembling fingers touched hers. Megan clasped her sister's wrist. "Roxy! Hold on. I'll pull you up."

Where she got the strength to heave the younger girl over the lip of the muddy, undercut bank she didn't know. Everything happened in a blur. Roxanne shot up out of the riverbed as if jumping from a trampoline and landed with a thump and a whimper.

Megan tearfully gathered her into an embrace. "Oh, honey. We thought we'd lost you!"

"Me, too," the girl said, clinging and shivering. "Oh, Meg, I'm so sorry."

"It's okay. It's over. You're safe now."

Pushing herself away, Roxy shook her head so violently, droplets of water scattered. "No. It's not over. Zac's still down there."

"Don't worry. James—Mr. Harris will bring him up in a minute."

"But he's hurt."

Megan's heart lumped in her throat. "James? How—?"

"No, Zac. He was wonderful, Meg. I thought he was just a kid but you should have seen him. He…"

Megan grasped the girl's shoulders. "What happened to Zac? How badly is he injured?"

"I don't know. I think maybe his leg is broken. Mr. Harris said he'd have to carry him."

This news changed everything. Megan eyed the thin leather reins. How much weight could they bear before snapping under the strain? She gritted her teeth. Reins, nothing. How much strain could her *nerves* take before snapping?

"I prayed and prayed," Roxy said between sniffles, tremors and jerky breaths.

Taking off the plastic poncho, Megan slipped it over her sister's head. "Don't stop now," she told the girl. "Only two of us are safe. James and Zac still need all the extra help they can get."

"I won't let you pack me around like some baby," Zac declared.

James would have worried more if he hadn't sensed fear behind the boy's bravado. "Fine. Well, guess I'll be going. See ya."

"Wait! You can't leave me here!"

"I don't intend to stick around till I lose my chance of escape. And you won't let me help you, so—"

"Okay, okay. But if you tell the other kids about this I'll, I'll…"

"I don't intend to say one word, except to the police."

"Police? I didn't do nothin'."

"We'll talk about that later," James said firmly. "Right now, you and I have to figure out how we're going to get out of this mess. Any ideas?"

"You said you were going to carry me."

"Only if you're sure you can hang on no matter what happens. There's a chance we may fall into the river. If we got separated in the water you could be in real trouble."

"Like I'm not already?" Zac made a face. "You're gonna hand me over to the cops."

"I never said that. But somebody has some serious explaining to do. A lot of folks have been out searching for you and your girlfriend."

"Girlfriend? Yeah, right," Zac said. "She might make an okay nurse but she's a lousy date. All she did was complain. And it was her fault we were out here."

"I said, we'll discuss it later." James lifted the youth to his feet and steadied him, then turned and crouched down. "Put your arms around my neck. When I stand up, I'll grab your knees. You know. Like playing piggyback."

"I've seen it."

But you never had a daddy to give you rides, did

you? James thought. *Of course not.* So many simple things like that were taken for granted by anyone who'd had a so-called normal childhood. Even he remembered enjoyable outings with his parents, especially when he was very young. To children like those who were placed in Camp Refuge, that kind of life must seem like an unattainable dream.

He straightened, his hands on the boy's forearms where they passed around his neck. "I'm knotting the cuffs of that jacket together to help you hang on. Ready?"

"Uh, yeah. I guess so."

James carried him to the entrance and paused. The only way he could use the rope for assistance was to let go of Zac's legs. Whether the injured one was broken or not, pain would keep the youth from gripping with it.

"Hang on a minute," James said. "I'll tie the shoelaces on your bad foot to my belt so your leg won't wobble around too much, in case I have to let go. Think you can stand it like that?"

"I can stand anything."

"Yeah. You're tough. I forgot." And a scared kid, too, he reminded himself. "Listen, Zac, if there was any other way…"

"Just get me out of here, okay?"

"Okay."

Eyeing the water mere inches from his feet, James steadied the boy's bad leg and reached for the lifeline. Megan was waiting for him at the other end.

In a way, she was his lifeline, too. All he had to do was reach her.

"I see them!" Roxy yelled. "They're almost to the top."

Rain had ceased to fall. Excess water dripped sporadically from the trees. Megan was using the flashlight to check the condition of the bridle, praying that their improvised rescue rig would hold. She shined the weakening beam at the buckles that held the reins to the bit. That connection seemed secure, yet something about it bothered her. If only she could see more clearly.

Though she wanted to be at the brink of the riverbank to greet James, something held her back. She put out her hand. Touched one of the rings on either side of the bit. There was a barely perceptible movement. An instant later, the upper rein broke away!

Amazingly, Megan's fingers were in the right place at the right time. She caught the loose bridle, dropping the flashlight so she could use both hands, and held on for dear life.

Skidding toward the edge of the embankment like a water-skier being pulled behind a speedboat, she tried to dig her heels into the wet ground.

Roxy lunged as she sailed past, grabbing her and knocking her down. Together, they were dragged across the soggy, uneven forest floor. A scrub oak came between them, halting their slide just short of disaster.

Roxy spit leaves. "Phew! What happened?"

"One of the reins broke. Are you okay?"

"Yeah. You?"

"So far. Whatever you do, *don't let go!*"

From below they heard a shout. "Megan, give me a hand. There's something wrong with this rope."

"I know. Sorry. Can you make it on your own? We're tied up right now."

To her great relief, he poked his head above the precipice. "What the…?"

"Don't ask," Megan said. "Just get on up here so we can relax, will you? My arms are cramping."

James grabbed a cedar sapling and used it to pull himself the rest of the way. "Okay. You can let go," he told her. "We're on solid ground."

Collapsing with relief, Megan watched him untie Zac, swing him around to the front and lower him gently. The boy was perspiring profusely and his eyes glistened. She suspected James was also trying to suppress tears of gratitude. She certainly was.

She and her sister were still prostrate beneath the bushy oak, gasping from their efforts, when James dropped to his knees beside her. "Are you all right?"

"I'm fine. Now," Megan said. "You're here."

She reached to caress his beloved face. A smile blossomed. Unashamed of her tears, she let him help her to her feet without protest and stepped into his embrace as if she'd done so a million times before.

James clasped her tight for long seconds, then held her away to gaze into her misty eyes. "I can't believe you two stopped that line the way you did. You're amazing. I owe you, big-time. "

"Well, I don't know about *her*," Megan said, eyeing her waterlogged sister, "but you owe me plenty."

Roxy made a sound of unmistakable disgust as she crawled out from under the bush and struggled to her feet. "Hey, don't worry about me, you guys. I'm just peachy. Not hurt a bit. And I can get up all by myself. Don't need any help. No sir."

Oblivious to the younger girl's sarcasm, James looked fondly at Megan and spoke softly. "I meant it. I do owe you a lot."

"Good. You can start by paying me off with a decent kiss—for a change."

"Oh?" His eyebrows arched. "You have complaints about my kisses?"

"How would I know? They happen so fast it's a wonder I even noticed."

"You noticed."

Her grin grew so broad her cheeks ached. "Oh, yeah? Prove it."

James whispered, "Gladly," and touched his lips to hers. This time he lingered.

In the background, Zac gave a theatrical groan. "Oh, brother."

Roxy giggled. "Quiet, you blockhead. This is s-o-o-o romantic."

It took a few moments for the youngsters' words to penetrate the fog of love and happiness surrounding Megan. When she did become aware of their candid comments, she made up her mind to ignore them. That was a mistake. The harder she tried, the funnier everything seemed.

Already at the end of her ability to cope, she lost control and burst into laughter. She roared. Chortled. Guffawed. Giggled. And generally made a fool of herself.

That didn't stop her. Nothing did. She simply

had to laugh, tears streaming down her face, until she was too spent to continue.

"I—I'm sorry," she finally blurted.

"No problem," James replied. "I'll just keep trying new techniques till I get it right."

The silly expression on his face set her off again. This time she regained control faster. "It was a wonderful kiss. Honest. But I certainly don't mind if you want to practice some more."

"Later," James said. "It's almost dawn. I want to get back to camp before everybody wakes up and starts worrying for nothing."

"Good idea." Megan pointed to Zac and her sister. "So, how are we going to handle those two? They aren't heavy, but I can't see fitting four people on Buckets."

"Three, at the most," James declared. "I don't care what you decide to do. I'm walking."

"I probably am, too. If we can't repair the bridle, I'll have to lead her, especially since we need to pick a smooth path home so we don't disturb Zac's leg."

James sighed. "Yeah. He's been through a lot."

"So has Roxy."

"Does this mean you don't think we should throttle them?" An eyebrow arched to emphasize that he was teasing.

"Not yet. Let's get them back to civilization first," Megan said with a sweet smile. "Then we'll sit them down under really bright lights and badger them with questions till they break." She giggled. "You did order extra vials of truth serum, didn't you?"

"Okay, okay. You've made your point. I'm glad to have them back, too. But how do you propose we find out what really happened?"

"Oh, I don't know," she drawled. "Hey, here's a novel idea. What do you say we *ask* them?"

"You are an optimist, aren't you?"

"Uh-huh. And you should be thankful for it. Anybody else might have figured it was no use and let go of that bridle when the rein snapped."

"I know. I thought for sure the kid and I were going for a swim. I can't imagine where you found the strength to hang on long enough for me to get my feet back under me. It's amazing."

"Oh, I think it's a lot more than that," Megan told him with a deep sigh. "It's almost miraculous."

Riding alone, Zac said very little as they headed for Camp Refuge. Roxy, on the other hand, trotted beside Megan and jabbered incessantly.

"I didn't know Zac was watching me or I'd

have waited," the girl said. "He followed me out of camp, giving me a lecture like he was my boss or something."

"What were you doing out in the woods alone in the first place?" Megan asked.

"Well, duh. Running away, of course."

"But why? Where did you think you could go?"

Roxy waved her scratched, dirty hands in the air. "I don't know. It didn't matter then. I just wanted to get away, so I left."

"You didn't care how worried I'd be, did you?"

"No." Roxy's brashness faded. "I didn't mean to hurt anybody. Especially you, Meg. I'm sorry."

"What about Zac?" Megan asked. "What happened to him?"

She hadn't thought the boy was paying any attention to their conversation till he interrupted with, "I fell. That's all."

"It is not," Roxy insisted. "He saved my life. There was this big snake. I almost stepped right on it. Zac pushed me out of the way and knocked me down. We missed the snake but we landed in a heap."

"That's when he hurt his leg?"

Nodding, Roxy had tears in her eyes. "Yes. By that time I was real lost. We both were. I couldn't just run off and leave him."

"Of course you couldn't. What happened then?"

"We decided we'd spend the night under a bunch of leaves, only Zac got really cold. I gave him my jacket—I mean your jacket—but it wasn't enough. We were trying to move out of the wind when we saw a place to hide."

"The cave where we found you."

"Uh-huh. It was warmer in there. I gathered wood and Zac told me how to make a fire. We thought maybe his leg would get better if we rested so we sort of made camp."

"What about food?"

"I had some candy bars and a bottle of water with me. We got real thirsty. Finally I took the empty bottle down to the river and tried to scoop up some clean water." She made a sour face. "You should have seen that awful stuff. Zac used his T-shirt to strain out the bugs."

"Sounds like he was using his head."

Blushing, Roxy grinned. "I know. Isn't he wonderful?"

Megan had been leading Buckets while James walked behind and to the side to look after Zac. She glanced over her shoulder in time to see the man give the youngster a smile and a proud pat on his good knee.

Silently rejoicing, she marveled over how ev-erything had worked out for the best. Funny how the worst circumstances could turn around that way, wasn't it? The tough smart-aleck who had delighted in causing trouble had been given the chance to use his wits for good and had proven more than worthy. And the self-centered teen with a chip on her shoulder had sacrificed her own comfort and safety to care for an injured com-panion. What a blessing!

And James? Megan smiled. James had proba-bly changed the most. He'd mellowed unbelieva-bly for starters. It was going to be a pleasure to complete her animal therapy project, knowing she now had his full support.

And after that was over? The smile spread into a wide grin. Afterward, maybe they could com-bine their efforts and find a way to work together continually. It gave her goose bumps just to think of spending every day with a wonderful, support-ive man like James Harris.

James was not only intelligent and compassion-ate, he now had a whole life of God-given glad-ness and amazing surprises ahead of him. A life she planned to share.

Megan giggled as her thoughts focused on spe-cifics. Her lips tingled. There were lots of reasons

why she wanted to spend the rest of her life with
James, and the kiss he'd recently given her was
right at the top of her list.

Chapter Fifteen

By the time Megan led Buckets back into camp the place was buzzing with morning activity. She and James were immediately surrounded by adults and children, everyone yammering at once.

James lifted a tearful Bobby Joe and placed him astride the horse behind his big brother, cautioning the child to be careful not to bump into Zac's injured leg.

As soon as James was certain both boys were safely settled for their happy reunion, he raised his hand to bring order and spoke with authority. "Okay. Let's get organized. Aaron, you call the sheriff. Tell him we've found the kids and have him send an ambulance for them. Zac's got a leg that needs attention. I want Roxy to go along and be checked out, too. They both drank untreated river water."

"Yes, sir." Aaron pulled James aside to speak to him privately, then left to follow the director's orders.

James was all business when he turned toward Megan. "You'll need to go along and look after your sister, at least until one of your parents shows up."

"Of course, but…" She glanced in the direction of her cabin. "I don't know if I can get all my animals fed and watered and wash the mud out of my hair in time to ride in the ambulance."

"There probably won't be room for passengers, anyway. Aaron can drive you to the hospital if you're not ready to leave here when I am. I'll need to sign a release before they'll treat Zac. There's no rush with Roxy."

"Okay." Megan smiled at her bedraggled sister. "I suppose letting her take a shower and change before she leaves is out of the question?"

"I doubt there'll be time. I'll give her and Zac a little to eat and drink while we wait. Can't give them too much right away. It might make them sick."

Megan steadied Buckets while James helped Bobby Joe dismount, followed by Zac. The older boy gritted his teeth but didn't cry out as James carefully cradled him.

Rushing to Zac, Roxy grabbed the boy's hand, fussing and cooing as if she were his mother. "Don't worry. You'll be fine. I'll stay with you, just like before. I promise."

Megan was waiting for James to say something else to her. She didn't expect him to express his personal feelings in front of the staff and the children, but she was hoping for a kind word or at least a smile of encouragement.

Instead, he merely turned and carried the injured child through the crowd of onlookers without even bidding Megan a casual goodbye.

Aaron showed up at Megan's campsite a few minutes later and volunteered to help with chores.

"Just tell me what to do. I can take care of everything while you grab a shower," he said.

"There's only Wiggles left to feed. I'll do that. His food's inside anyway. Would you mind rinsing out all the water pails and refilling them with clean drinking water?"

"No problem. Mr. Harris just left. Soon as you're ready we'll head for the hospital, too. Might even beat the ambulance, slow as they are sometimes."

"Oh. Well, I suppose there's no rush. Zac hurt himself a couple of days ago." She yawned. "It seems like a lot longer. I feel like I haven't slept a wink since, oh, maybe last November."

Aaron chuckled. "That's how Mr. Harris looks, too. I've never seen him so beat."

"It was a *really* long night."

"Yeah. I gathered."

Something in the young man's tone gave her pause. "For the record, between the storm, the river, rescuing the kids and bringing everybody safely home, we didn't have time to mess around. Understand?"

"That's what he said, too."

"You don't sound like you believe us."

The young man shrugged. "Doesn't matter what I do or don't believe. Harris is cooked. I just hope I can find another part-time job this summer."

"What do you mean?"

"Camp Refuge is closing down."

"What? When?"

"Soon as possible, or so I heard."

"Does James know?"

"He does now. I just told him."

"When we first got here." It wasn't a question. No wonder James had suddenly become so preoccupied, so distant. Who wouldn't be? His life's work was being terminated, yet all she'd been thinking about was herself. Roxy wasn't the only one with a few lessons to learn, was she?

"Yeah," Aaron said. "He didn't act nearly as upset as I thought he'd be. Guess he'd seen it coming. It figures, especially after—"

Megan scowled when he broke off. "After what?"

"Nothing."

"Oh, no, you don't. Finish what you started. Why would James not be surprised?"

"You ought to know."

"Me? What do I have to do with this?"

"I can't say."

Frustration banished her weariness. "Fine. Have it your way. Just don't disappear on me, okay? I'll be cleaned up and ready to go by the time you finish watering my animals."

"Yes, ma'am."

Muttering to herself, Megan did an about-face and ran for the cabin. She didn't know exactly what had happened to put an end to Camp Refuge but she had a strong suspicion Zac's disappearance had been the last straw. If that were the case, Roxy had been directly responsible.

And Megan shared the guilt.

The redbrick facade was the most impressive part of the tiny rural hospital. Everything else was painted a sickly pale green. Aaron drove Megan around to the emergency entrance and let her out by the concrete ramp.

"Thanks for the ride."

"Welcome. Want me to wait?" he asked cheerfully.

"No. You're still needed back at camp. Inez can't do it all."

"In a few days she'll be able to. John and Robbie are leaving tomorrow. Mark's supposed to go to a foster home then, too."

Megan paused and leaned in the passenger-side window. "What about Kyle?"

"Already gone."

"They didn't waste any time, did they?"

"Guess not. I heard you might have some pull with the board. That true?"

"I used to think so," she said pensively.

"Well, in case I don't see you again, good luck."

"Thanks. And thanks for the information— what little there was of it."

"Hey," he said, grinning and raising his hands as if surrendering, "I didn't tell you a thing."

Megan couldn't help but chuckle. By not revealing certain details of the camp closure, he'd told her more than enough. She sobered. Whether James Harris liked it or not, she intended to dig until she learned the whole truth. Then she'd go to work making amends for all the trouble she'd inadvertently caused. By presenting justification for James's actions to the board of directors and placing the blame on herself, where it belonged, there was a fair chance she could get him reinstated.

She huffed in disgust. Convincing the board that Camp Refuge was a valuable asset shouldn't be as hard as explaining Roxy's latest misadventure to their skeptical parents. What fun *that* was going to be.

The moment she entered the hospital waiting room, Megan's attention centered on James. Though there were several others in the room, he was seated apart, his head bent, his shoulders slumped, his elbows resting on his knees, hands folded.

She approached slowly and stopped in front of him. *What should I say?* Nothing earth-shattering came to mind. Nothing helpful did, either.

Softly she breathed only his name. "James?"

He looked up, gave her a brief smile and pointed. "Your sister's in exam room three. Your mother's with her."

"Mom's here already? Uh-oh. That was fast. How did she and Roxy seem?"

"If you mean were they yelling at each other? No. It's probably safe for you to join them."

"They'll be better off without me. Besides, I didn't come here to see my crazy family," Megan said, taking the empty seat next to him. "I came here to be with you."

His head snapped around. "Why?"

"Maybe I like grumpy men."

"Well, you're in the right place for that. I take it you heard what's happening to Camp Refuge."

"I heard a little. I'd like the whole story from your point of view."

James shook his head and went back to staring at the floor. "There's not much to tell."

"Then let me guess. You'd mentioned something about too many disciplinary problems. When Zac ran off after Roxy, I assume you caught a lot of flack, especially since we had to call in the sheriff. Is that why they're pulling the plug?"

"Close enough."

"I'm so sorry. How can I help?" To her relief, he didn't resist when she reached for his hand. Instead, he laced their fingers together before he answered.

"You can't help. Nobody can."

"I can talk to the board for you. Tell them it was all my fault. They'll have to listen."

"No. I don't want you to beg. I gave it my best. It's over. Time to move on."

"You're quitting?"

James squeezed her hand as he shook his head, smiling. "Oh, no. Not in a million years. I'll just find another way—a better way—to help troubled kids."

He paused, studying her expression. "I've been sitting here, trying to decide how best to do that."

"And?" Megan's heart was thumping so loud she felt like the drum section in a marching band.

"And I thought maybe you and I should join forces. We could combine our expertise, write a program together and apply for new funding. What do you think?"

"I think it's a wonderful idea!"

"You hadn't considered it before?"

"Me? Perish the thought," Megan teased. She gave a nervous laugh. "Actually, I haven't been able to think of anything *but* working with you. We'll make a great team."

"We sure will."

"And because there are two of us, the family dynamics will be much better." Elated, she was warming to her subject and dropping her guard. "We'll be just like a real parents, 24/7."

James coughed. His eyes widened. "Whoa. Did you just propose to me?"

"Uh-oh." A lump of embarrassment the size of Buckets clogged her throat. "I—I thought that was what we were talking about. Oh, dear." She jerked her hand free and headed for the door.

James jumped to his feet, grabbed her and spun her around to face him. "Hold on. Don't you want my answer?"

"Only if you're going to say yes."

He beamed. His eyes sparkled. "Tell you what. Let's do it this way. I'll ask you to marry me, too. Then we can both say yes at the same time."

"Yes!" she blurted out in a loud voice.

Every person in the room froze and stared at them.

Laughing, James took her in his arms. "You in a hurry, lady?"

"I guess I am. You don't mind, do you?"

"Not at all. I was going to wait a while before I brought up the subject of marriage, but as long as you're sure we're not moving too fast, it's okay with me. I can't believe how ready I am to settle down all of a sudden."

"Me, too."

"Just one little promise before we set the date."

"Oh?" She eyed his wry, comical expression and speculated. "The squirrel stays."

"It's not about Rocky."

"Wiggles sleeps on the floor in my bedroom."

"That's fine, too."

"Then what? *What?*"

"Horses," James told her, struggling to keep a straight face. "If we ever go on another rescue mission, I want you to promise me I won't have to ride a horse."

Megan giggled with relief and joy. "You don't want to be my knight in shining armor?"

"The shining armor is fine," he said, breaking into a wide grin. "I'd like nothing better than to be your hero for the rest of my life, as long as I get to do it with both feet on the ground."

"Well…" she drawled, "I've always dreamed of being married on horseback, sitting on a silver-mounted saddle, with my wedding dress spread out over the horse's rump, but if you insist…"

He looked so dismayed, she had to confess. "Relax. I was kidding."

"That weird sense of humor of yours is going to take some getting used to."

Megan stepped closer, slipped her arms around his waist and laid her cheek against his chest.

"Don't worry. We have the rest of our lives to figure each other out."

"I'm looking forward to it." He tilted her chin up with one finger and gazed into her eyes.

Just before she reached on tiptoe to kiss him she said, "Me, too. I can hardly wait to get started."

Epilogue

Megan's heart was filled to the brim with love for the handsome man waiting for her at the far end of the aisle. She couldn't have asked for a more perfect day, or a more beautiful setting, for an outdoor wedding.

A slight breeze lifted the edges of her veil and ruffled her hair. Change was in the air. Soon, the Ozarks would be awash with the bright colors of fall. And even sooner, she would be Mrs. James Harris.

Her mother had helped her into her long white dress, then kissed her before going to sit in the front row of folding chairs next to Roxy. The girl had wisely placed herself as a buffer between their parents, allowing their father and his new wife and son to sit on her other side. James's family had sent polite regrets.

Breaking with tradition, Megan had asked Zac to give her away, much to everyone's astonishment—including Zac's. She'd been afraid he was going to turn her down until James had offered to take him shopping for clothes and shoes and had also promised to coach him so he wouldn't make any mistakes in etiquette.

As an added blessing, Zac and Bobby Joe had been placed in James's custody until a suitable, two-parent home could be found for them. Megan had every intention of becoming their mother as soon as possible, her first move being to marry their foster daddy as a prelude to filing necessary adoption papers.

Megan held tight to Zac's arm and waited for the service to begin. The boy looked amazingly suave and fully composed, though he still had a slight limp.

"You okay, Ms. Megan?" he whispered.

"Sure. Just scared to death," she answered softly.

"Hey, don't worry. Mr. Harris'll catch you if you faint or something."

"I'm not going to faint."

The boy exhaled noisily and wiggled his eyebrows. "Whew! That's a relief."

She couldn't help but be amused at his antics.

"Behave yourself, mister. Getting married is serious. If you make me laugh, we're both going to be in trouble."

"No kidding it's serious," Zac said. "I never figured on wearing a suit, ever. This tie's about to strangle me."

"Zac…"

"Okay, okay. That lady over there's waving at us to go. You ready?"

"Ready." Megan looked down at the boy and smiled. There was something about his grin that gave her pause. She scowled. "What's up? You look funny."

"Nothing's up," he said, all innocence.

"Then take your other hand out of your coat pocket and stand up straight like James showed you."

"Can't," the boy said. "Rocky's getting kind of restless. I wouldn't want him to run away."

After her worrisome trip down the aisle with Zac—and the hidden flying squirrel—Megan was more than glad to be with James instead. As their reception line was forming, she quietly told her new husband about the uninvited wedding guest dozing in Zac's pocket.

"That little stinker," James said, chuckling.

"Who? Rocky or Zac?"

"Zac. I made him promise a lot of things before today but I didn't think to ask him to leave out the animals."

"It's okay. It could have been a lot worse."

"The way that squirrel takes to you, it sure could have." He laughed softly. "Would have made a good shot for the family album, though. Real unforgettable."

James reached into his inside jacket pocket. "Speaking of forgetting. I almost forgot to show you this. Gray handed it to me right before the service. It's our wedding present from him and Stacy."

"That's nice, I—"

Megan gasped and almost dropped her bridal bouquet when James unfolded the paper. It was the deed to the Camp Refuge property. "They gave us this? Just *gave* it to us? I didn't know they were rich. They seem so normal. Why didn't you tell me?"

"Because I never think of them as being different. Gray's just my old friend. Has been for years. Most of the time, I forget he's loaded."

"Do you realize what this means? We can re-open Camp Refuge ourselves instead of having to look all over for another place to work."

"I know." Pensive, he refolded the deed and slipped it back into his jacket pocket. "I can hardly believe it."

"I can." Megan beamed. "It's the answer to our prayers."

"You think so?"

"Don't you? Sure looks like it to me."

"I don't know. I'm still pretty confused about all this spiritual stuff. To be honest, I'd expected my life to run a lot more smoothly once I got tuned in to God. It sure hasn't worked that way. Seems like things are even more hectic than before."

Megan gave him a loving smile. "I hate to break this to you, but our faith gets tested all the time. That's one way we grow."

"*Now* you tell me."

She laughed at his feigned expression of dismay and patted his hand. "Don't worry, honey. Now that we're married, we can start getting into trouble as a team."

James pulled her close and kissed her, much to the delight of their assembled guests, then whispered, "I can hardly wait."

* * * * *

Dear Reader,

The Scripture I chose to inspire this story is sometimes hard to accept or understand. Many times, new Christians falter because they mistakenly believe that once they turn their lives over to Christ, their problems will cease. That's seldom the case. However, those of us who have been believers for a longer time have seen how God shepherds us through the hardest, most trying circumstances, always providing the solace we need.

Look for joy in everything. Celebrate the life He has given you. Do the best you can to use your special talents (yes, we all have them) and give thanks even when you don't understand why your plans haven't worked out the way you'd hoped. God knows what He's doing. If you belong to Him, trust Him. If you're questioning whether or not you're truly His child, all you have to do is surrender your pride, ask Him to forgive and accept you right now and He will. It's that easy.

I love to hear from readers. The quickest replies are by e-mail—VALW@CENTURYTEL.NET— or you can write to me at P.O. Box 13, Glencoe, AR 72539, and I'll do my best to answer as soon as I can spare time away from my latest manuscript. And www.centurytel.net/valeriewhisenand will take you to my Internet site.

Blessings,

Valerie Hansen

From #1 CBA bestselling and
Christy Award-winning author

DEE HENDERSON

comes her first classic romance.

As Scott Williams's thirty-eighth birthday dawned, he was at the top of his game.
Or was he? Successful, blessed with friends and a rich faith, his life seemed perfect to others. But something was missing—a family of his own to love.

After making a birthday wish to meet the woman of his dreams, Scott encountered
enchanting author Jennifer St. James strolling along the beach. But beneath her
beauty lay a heart mourning her late husband and a faith once deep, now fragile.
Could Scott's hopes and prayers bring fulfillment for both of their dreams?

*"Henderson has steadily built a name for herself...
intriguing...insightful and probing."*
—*Publishers Weekly*

Available in September 2004.

Steeple
Hill®

www.SteepleHill.com

SDH519

Take 2 inspirational love stories FREE!

PLUS get a FREE surprise gift!

Mail to Steeple Hill Reader Service™

In U.S.
3010 Walden Ave.
P.O. Box 1867
Buffalo, NY 14240-1867

In Canada
P.O. Box 609
Fort Erie, Ontario
L2A 5X3

YES! Please send me 2 free Love Inspired® novels and my free surprise gift. After receiving them, if I don't wish to receive anymore, I can return the shipping statement marked cancel. If I don't cancel, I will receive 4 brand-new novels every month, before they're available in stores! Bill me at the low price of $4.24 each in the U.S. and $4.74 each in Canada, plus 25¢ shipping and handling and applicable sales tax, if any*. That's the complete price and a savings of over 10% off the cover prices—quite a bargain! I understand that accepting the books and gift places me under no obligation ever to buy any books. I can always return a shipment and cancel at any time. Even if I never buy another book from Steeple Hill, the 2 free books and the surprise gift are mine to keep forever.

113 IDN DZ9M
313 IDN DZ9N

Name	(PLEASE PRINT)
Address	Apt. No.
City	State/Prov.	Zip/Postal Code

Not valid to current Love Inspired® subscribers.

Want to try two free books from another series?
Call **1-800-873-8635** or visit **www.morefreebooks.com.**

* Terms and prices are subject to change without notice. Sales tax applicable in New York. Canadian residents will be charged applicable provincial taxes and GST. All orders subject to approval. Offer limited to one per household.

® are registered trademarks owned and used by the trademark owner and or its licensee.

INTLI04R   ©2004 Steeple Hill

Love Inspired

GOLD IN THE FIRE

BY

MARGARET DALEY

A string of burning barns worried firefighter Joshua Markham—his quiet town, Sweetwater, was at the mercy of a serial arsonist. Yet it was a beautiful woman trying to save her family's horses that took his breath away. Darcy O'Brien and her young son needed a chance to start over, but neither Joshua nor Darcy was ready for a relationship, as their respective pasts had left them wary. But when the arsonist struck close to home, would Joshua risk everything for the woman he loved?

Don't miss

GOLD IN THE FIRE

On sale October 2004

Available at your favorite retail outlet.

www.SteepleHill.com

LIGITFMD